The Way Out

A collection of short stories

Vicki Jarrett

FREIGHT BOOKS

Vicki Jarrett lives and works in her native Edinburgh. Her first novel, Nothing is Heavy, was shortlisted for the Saltire Society First Book of the Year 2013. Her short fiction has been widely published and broadcast, shortlisted for the Scotland on Sunday/ Macallan Short Story Competition, Manchester Fiction Prize and Bridport Prize. The Way Out is her first collection.

First published 2015

Freight Books
49-53 Virginia Street
Glasgow, G1 1TS
www.freightbooks.co.uk

A CIP catalogue reference for this book is available from the British Library.

ISBN 978-1-910449-02-8
eISBN 978-1-910449-03-5

Typeset by Freight in Plantin
Printed and bound by Bell and Bain, Glasgow

the publisher acknowledges investment from
Creative Scotland toward the publication of this book

Contents

This book is dedicated to all those who dream of escape.

Something Wrong

Today the papergirl delivers the news to the big houses. She folds her body into the wind to make herself narrow, so she can slip through the gaps in the rain. The bag of papers slung across her shoulder bumps off the back of her legs as she walks, turning her progress into a battle against turbulence. Sometimes she regrets taking this job, but she's not sorry to miss the morning routine at home.

This isn't her usual round but at least she can't get lost on this one. One single road. Must be about a mile long but all she has to do is go all the way down one side and all the way back up the other. She doesn't have to deal with the tangled geography of the estate.

Her original route was a nightmare. She couldn't seem to get the streets in the right order. She was always having to double back on herself, trailing around terraces, crescents and cul-de-sacs that made no sense to her. It took her so long to complete the deliveries that there were complaints and she was often late for school. Mister Patterson, the newsagent, was patient at first because he was short-staffed. He must've assumed she'd get quicker with experience, but this morning he'd said, 'Last chance. If you can't get this round done in under an hour, I'll have to let you go.' Fair enough. He didn't shout or try to make her feel stupid.

Whichever part of the brain is supposed to be in charge of a sense of direction does not exist in the brain of the papergirl. Or perhaps she has a wonky chromosome. They did that in biology last term. How everything like hair and eye colour and pointless stuff like whether you can roll your tongue is coded into your DNA. There is something wrong with her code.

Left and right have always been a problem, as long as she can remember. Close up, they're fine. She knows her own right and left hands, can put her shoes on her right and left feet. No problem there. But as soon as she starts trying to apply direction to the world around her, it all falls apart. She remembers, in primary school, she tried to explain her doubts and the teacher had another child stand facing her. They'd squared up to each other, hands dropped to their sides, fingers curled and twitching around their own loaded ideas of left and right. She was outgunned. If they were both right, both correct, as the teacher insisted, then that meant every direction was both left and right at the same time. What use was that in finding your way?

She crosses the road and starts back on the return leg. The traffic is heavier now, heading into town. She'll have to watch her time. Provided the road doesn't start tying itself in knots ahead of her, she should make it. The houses are large and set back from the road by gardens with driveways, trees and dark bushes that throw handfuls of rainwater at her as she passes, feet crunching over gravel. Only a few of the houses are still family homes, most have been converted into offices or split up into flats.

About half way along she comes to one with a nameplate that says Sunshine House. Despite the cartoon smiley sun above the name, the place doesn't look very sunny. The stone front is dark with rain, its narrow windows reflect the morning's grey skies. The letterbox is vertical and spring-loaded, unwilling. Soon the outer pages of the *Independent* she's trying to force through start to crumple and tear. She gives up and rings the bell. They'll probably complain less about being disturbed than finding a shredded newspaper on their doorstep.

She's not prepared for the full-frontal assault that barrels into her when the door opens. The force of it nearly knocks her off her feet and she stammers over her words as she holds out the paper. She's not sure if the owner of the friendliest smile she's ever seen is male or female, or how old they might be. They're shorter than her and softly plump. Before she can wonder at this, her spare hand is grasped and she is tugged over the threshold and into the house. She experiences a brief moment of alarm when the door closes behind her but no sense of threat as she is led by the hand into a large kitchen filled with half a dozen more smiling faces.

A chorus of cheers goes up. Somebody hugs her. A strong hug, arms wrapped tightly around her waist, head buried in her chest. She holds her arms up and out to the side, completely bewildered. They must be mistaking her for someone else, someone who looks like her perhaps. She should explain about the paper. But the hug is so warm and tight, so generous, that eventually she lowers her arms. Everyone cheers again. Someone offers her a bowl of cereal. 'Have some coco pops!'

The kitchen is warm, the steamed-up windows striped with runs of condensation. A long table covered with a yellow, plastic tablecloth is cluttered with cereal boxes and mismatched cups and bowls. She feels dizzy and thinks she might faint but that it would be okay if she did. She starts to laugh and the more she laughs, the happier everyone gets until the kitchen is a hubbub of laughter and excitement. Some huge unfamiliar sensation is rising through her body, filling her up to the brim. Someone reaches up, pats at her face with a dishcloth and tells her, 'You are raining, silly!'

The laughter dies down and she looks up to see a middle-aged man with a patchy beard and a bottle-green cardigan standing in the doorway peering at her through wire-rimmed

3

glasses. 'What's going on here?'

She swallows and steadies herself, explains about the paper, holds up her bag.

'Oh dear, not again,' sighs the man. 'Christine, didn't I tell you?' he says to the person who opened the door. 'You mustn't keep kidnapping people!'

She doesn't want to leave but knows there isn't any reason they should let her stay. She peels herself away from the hugs and allows the man to escort her out. Everyone follows them to the door, waves and smiles, smiles and waves. And then she's out, back into the wind and the rain. She tries to fold herself into them again but can't seem to fit. She walks for five, ten, maybe fifteen minutes before she realises she's going in the wrong direction.

The next day the papergirl delivers the news to the breakfast table.

'You got sacked? From a paper round?' Her father makes a rare appearance from behind his newspaper.

Her brother snorts and shakes his head in amazement. She has once again managed to surprise him with just how useless she can be.

She tries to tell the story of Sunshine House, tries to describe the warmth of it.

Her mother frowns and interrupts. 'What were you thinking of, going in there?' she says. 'It could've been dangerous.'

She shakes her head. 'No...'

'You actually went *inside* Sunshine House?' Her brother grins in an ugly, lopsided way.

'So what?'

'It's a *home*.' The way her mother says the word has an inflection to it, a lowering of tone and a pressing down on the o-sound that somehow completely changes the meaning. 'For folk with something wrong with them.'

'You'd fit right in there,' says her brother, laughing. 'Ya mong.'

Her mother bangs her mug down and coffee splashes onto the table. 'Richard!'

Her father silently folds over a page of his newspaper and lifts it back in front of his face as her mother and brother settle back into yelling at each other.

The papergirl focuses on the thin beam of sunlight stretched across the breakfast table, separating her from the rest of her family. 'There wasn't anything wrong with them.' But no one is listening. She pushes back her chair and leaves the room, leaves the house and starts walking. It doesn't matter which direction.

Worst Case Scenario

Hamid had one of the big knives and was holding it out towards me. 'Come here,' he said.

His face, as usual, was unreadable. My boss had a sour set to his mouth and narrow eyes that glittered with suppressed emotion. That was his normal look. I did my best to avoid finding out exactly which emotions he was suppressing. Behind him there was something frying on the griddle, strips of something dark sent up twisted spouts of metallic-smelling smoke.

'Try this.' He made a gesture with the knife which I realised was supposed to be reassuring. There was a sliver of cooked meat balanced on the flat of the blade.

I breathed out. 'What is it?'

Hamid often cooked up a little something private on the back grill. Ate it through the back with some watery yoghurt drink he kept in the fridge. He'd never touch a donner; said he didn't like Scottish food.

'Just try it.' He held the knife out towards me, nodding.

'No. Thanks. You're alright.' I didn't move.

He almost smiled, and tilted his head. 'Come on. I'm not trying to poison you.'

The meat behind him on the griddle shrank and hissed.

The kebabs we served were lamb or chicken, sometimes beef. We didn't sell anything with pork in it. Donner meat, a complete mystery to me before this job, turned out to be minced lamb, threaded in fat rounds over a metal rod and shaped into a tower of packed meat, cooked by rotating it in front of an upright grill.

I looked at the knife.

The shop was empty. I looked at the door and wished for a customer, or for Ali to come back from his break but the door stayed closed. I walked towards Hamid. I'm no longer vegetarian but that doesn't make me keen to experiment with unidentified bits of animal. But on balance I reckoned it'd be more dangerous to refuse. I asked myself, how bad could it be?

Col snorts with laughter when I get to this point in the story. So far he's hardly been listening. It's 2am and he's stretched out flat on the sofa, watching something on cable that involves a lot of pink flesh and squealing. I try not to focus on it.

'Worst case scenario?' he says.

I shrug. Typical Col to think it's up to him to supply the ending.

'It's dog, or cat or something,' he says. 'No, hang on, that's the Chinese, isn't it? What are that pair you work with?'

'They're from Iran.'

Ali and Hamid are brothers, although you'd never guess it to look at them. Ali came over when he was a kid, went to school here, calls me *hen* and *pet* and laughs easily. Apart from his silky black hair and dark eyes, he's hardly exotic. Hamid was already middle-aged when he arrived a year or so ago. Since then a wiry white tuft has appeared at his hairline and the lines around his mouth have deepened. He describes himself as Persian, doesn't talk much but when he does, his English, though accented, is faultless.

'Well then.'

'Well what?'

'You've no idea what he might be cooking up for you.'

'I do know.'

Col acts like I haven't spoken, distracted by a more interesting thought of his own. 'Oh! No. *Worst* case is it's human flesh.' He grins and nods, leans forward and puts on a pantomime scary whisper. 'He's killed someone and has the body stashed in the cellar and is using you to dispose of the evidence. Piece. By. Piece.'

'Don't be ridiculous.' Col watches too much telly. He thinks everything's some kind of show.

'It's not just anyone, either.' He stares at me and widens his eyes in a meaningful look. 'It's his brother.'

I sigh. Why did I even bother trying to tell Col about this? Why do I bother trying to tell him anything? 'Ali was on his break. He came back after.'

'Oh right.' Col is deflated but that lasts about a second till he comes up with another theory. 'Okay then. Even better. It's his wife.'

'He's not married.'

Col grins at me like we're playing some kind of a game and I'm giving him clues to solve. Listening is not one of his strong points.

'His mother!' He bounces on the sofa, sitting up now, pleased with himself. 'Yeah. Like Omar Bates or something. Iranian Psycho.' He sniggers and swills a mouthful of beer from the bottle in his hand.

'You're being childish.' Col isn't insulted, isn't listening anyway. I realise that being childish *is* one of his strong points, then wonder if it could really be described as such. I used to see it as playful and imaginative, liked his sense of fun. Now that feeling is being pushed out and something else is rushing in to fill up the empty space. I look at him, still in the same place I left him when I went to work, one hand down the front of his stained tracky bottoms, scratching his balls. I'm tired. My feet ache and I smell like kebabs. Maybe I'm hungry too. There's a half-eaten sausage roll on the table. I don't fancy it, although I've been eating meat again for some months, having slipped out of vegetarianism like an inconvenient skin. One of many.

'Oh god. No.' He slams the bottle down on the cluttered coffee table, wipes some foam from his lips. 'I've got it! It's his own flesh. He's cut it out of his thigh or his chest or something and he's bleeding under his clothes the whole time he's talking to you. Yeah.' Col lies back down and sighs, pleased he's solved my story to everyone's satisfaction. It's like I'm not even in the room any more. I'm starting to wish I wasn't and am just getting up to leave when Col starts laughing and chokes on his beer, waving the bottle at the TV. Eventually he spits out, 'It's the only way he can get his meat into your mouth!' before dissolving into helpless snorting giggles. I close my eyes, and the sound he's making merges with the muffled grunts from the television.

So weighing it all up, I took the piece of meat off the edge of the knife with my fingers.

'Careful. Very sharp knife.'

It was about the size and shape of a strip of gum and that's what I focused on as I popped it into my mouth and chewed. It was rich and dense but not fibrous, like super-concentrated paté. It wasn't so bad. Just meat. I swallowed and tried a smile.

'You going to tell me what it is now?'

'Did you like it?' Hamid was staring at me, his eyes greedy, looking me up and down like he expected something to happen, some kind of transformation.

I shrug. 'It was okay. What was it?'

'Heart.'

Generally I try not to guess at what's going on behind Hamid's eyes but right then I'd say it was a type of triumph, mixed with disgust.

'Really?' I ran my tongue over my teeth, picking up grains of ferric meaty residue.

'Yes.' He poked the remaining pieces on the grill, scooped another up with the knife and offered it to me.

'From what? What animal?'

He was looking at the meat, avoiding eye contact now. 'Pig,' he said, spitting out the single syllable like it might contaminate his mouth if he let it linger.

'No, thanks.' I try to keep my tone light, wondering all the same where Hamid got a pig's heart from. And why. 'I'm not really hungry. Why don't you have it?'

'I can't eat that.'

'Why not?' I thought that as long as we concentrated on the reasons he wasn't eating it then maybe we could avoid discussing why he wanted me to.

'If I eat this meat,' he hesitated, put the knife down. 'If a man puts this meat into his body, the blood from it will mix with his own blood and when it travels to his heart it will transform his heart to the heart of a pig.'

'What about a woman?'

He looked at me, his eyes glassy.

'You said if a *man* puts this meat into *his* body. What happens to a woman?'

He shrugged, dismissive, like it hardly mattered in that case.

'Where did you get it from?'

'Kevin. The butcher. When I buy the shop meat from him, sometimes he gives me things he has spare. Today it was this. I can't eat it. But I thought, maybe you…,' he trailed off as if unsure himself what he thought, as if the urge to take and cook this thing for me, to have me consume it, was something beyond his conscious control.

At that moment a customer pushed through the door, making the bell ring. Hamid flicked the remaining blackened scraps of meat from the grill into a paper wrapper and dropped it into the bin.

The rest of the evening went by with a constant stream of customers. Ali came back from his break and the three of us worked steadily, the column of donner meat reducing as slice after slice was shaved off and deposited in dozens of pitta breads, topped with salad and chilli sauce. By the end of the night it was shaved down to the metal spit.

Tidying up in the cellar after closing time with Hamid, the small space felt claustrophobic. He asked when me and Col were getting married.

'Not right now.'

'But you plan to marry?'

I glanced over at him. He was standing gazing upwards, longingly through the hatch of the cellar, back into the bright light of the shop as if looking at sunshine from behind prison bars.

He sighed and shook his head. 'Women here…' His face was sad and he looked at me with disappointment, his eyes asking how I could have let him down so badly.

'People live together. It's normal,' I told him, bristling a little. 'Gives them a chance to find out if they get on before having kids and all that. Even then, some couples never get married. It's no big deal.'

Hamid looked at me like I'd just told him the earth was flat. He reached one hand up towards the light. 'In my country, a woman is like a flower.'

I concentrated on gathering up some onions that had spilled out of a torn sack. I cast around for something, maybe some tape, to repair the rip and realised Hamid was looking at me, expecting a response.

'Oh?' The cellar walls contracted and I strained to hear the sound of Ali moving around upstairs, cleaning down the grills and mopping the floor.

'Once she is plucked,' Hamid made a mid-air snatching

motion with his outstretched hand and stared into my eyes, 'she dies.' He shrugged and turned away sorrowfully, started moving boxes around.

I wanted to ask him what he meant by that. Did he really believe I should just get on with it and die? My face grew hot. I felt my blood spewing through my veins, the pig blood working its way deeper in toward my centre, pushing fast in and out of my heart, the muscle swelling, coarsening, becoming an animal thing.

I undress and look at myself in the bedroom mirror. White flesh, raw on my bones. I drag an old t-shirt over my head and slide under the sheets. The sweaty soundtrack from the living room oozes through the crack in the door, punctuated by the tight pop of released air when Col opens another beer. The creak of the couch as he settles back down.

I can't sleep. The clock says 3.30am. I've been lying in bed for an hour, listening to the roar of blood in my ears. The blind pumping machinery of my heart, dense and dark, convulsing, the blood forced this way then that, under pressure from both sides.

I need to be moving. I throw off the sheets and pull my clothes back on, deciding to go for a walk. There's only an hour or so before dawn. In the living room, Col is sprawled with his mouth open, snoring. The TV is fuzzed with static, giving out a low whispering breath, like a never-ending exhalation.

Outside the sky is already lightening to the colour of a fading bruise, the air hanging cool and still, passive in the path of the coming day. I walk for maybe an hour through deserted streets, silent but for the drum of a thousand beating muscles behind stone walls, on and on, working while their owners sleep. I keep walking, my steps falling into rhythm with them, the world throbbing hypnotically under my feet.

There's an angry squeal of rubber on tarmac, followed by

the blast of a car horn and I realise I'm in the middle of the road. I raise my hands in apology to the driver. He's right up against his windscreen shouting, spit spraying from his mouth onto the glass. I back away, keeping an eye on him just in case he's thinking about getting out of his car. And that's when I make the same mistake again, jumping back onto the traffic island just in time. The truck stops right next to me, blocking my path and lets out a furious hiss like a red hot pan dropped into water.

The truck is huge with slatted sides. It smells of shit and something worse. The driver leans out of his window. 'Wake up, doll. I nearly had you there!'

I mutter my apologies and he disappears back inside.

From the body of the truck comes the scrape of shuffling feet. Through a gap in the side I see movement in the dark and suddenly a snout is pressed to the gap, wet and trembling, desperately snuffling the free air. Asking: are we here? Is this the place? It's so close I could touch it, this breathing, questioning thing. The truck rumbles and shakes as the driver throws it back into gear. The snout disappears back into the gloom but in its place comes an eye the colour of blood, framed by white eyelashes and creased pink skin. The pig looks right at me. It sees me and it knows. It knows I don't have the answer either.

The truck moves away, huffing exhaust fumes into the early morning air.

I know the slaughterhouse is nearby. Before long that heart will be silenced. The taste of it rises to my mouth like betrayal. I walk in the opposite direction, cross the road and sink down onto the low wall outside a supermarket. Delivery vans trundle into the car park, past a trough of parched geraniums and round to the back doors. The weight in my chest grows heavier and I think of the pig, freed from the truck, skidding unsteadily down the ramp to the holding pens, blinded by the sudden light that lies between.

What Remains

Standing by the sink in his kitchen, Marvin ran his hand under the cold tap until his finger bones ached like the roots of bad teeth. Was this to be the next thing then? Reduced to making tepid cups of tea to save himself from injury at his own shaking hand. He dabbed it dry with a cloth and examined the damage. There was a red scald the shape of Africa on the back of his left hand and it was beginning to hurt.

He looked out at the other houses lit in a golden haze from the streetlights. In the small upstairs bedroom of the house opposite, the pacing silhouette of a woman with a baby circled in the muted yellow light, round and round, like a sleepy goldfish. He pushed the window open a crack and listened to the child's cries rising and falling; a tiny human siren protesting the night.

Some days Marvin passed the mother in the street, her hair unwashed, narrow shoulders hunched. She looked like the stroller was the only thing holding her up. He'd offered to help her with her groceries once but she'd looked at him as if he'd volunteered to tap dance naked, and hurried into her house. Perhaps she didn't speak English. Considering how rarely folks around here spoke to each other these days, for all he knew they could each be speaking their own private languages.

Marvin didn't sleep a whole lot anymore. The small hours often found him in the kitchen, making tea to take back to bed. He still lay on the left hand side. The right retained Kath's shape, and although she hadn't filled it for over a decade now, when he woke with the scent of her around his face, the taste of her on his lips, he would reach into the empty space and find her gone all over again. After forty years together, what was left now but to miss her?

There was no point going back to the States. There was nothing there for him anymore, not even a decent cup of tea. At least here he could feel he was still with Kath, surrounded by what remained. This house. These memories. She used to joke he was her war bride. Instead of the pair of them shipping off to the States when they'd married after the war, she'd convinced him to make the move to her side of the Atlantic. Not that he'd put up much of a fight. He'd have moved to Timbuktu if that was what she'd wanted. They'd had a good life together. Children hadn't come along, which was a sadness, but they'd always had each other.

Sometimes the lack was like a great ragged hole in his guts, other times it was worse. He hadn't believed he could miss her more until yesterday when, for a whole horrifying minute, he had completely forgotten her name.

The memory gaps were happening more often now. At least he thought they were, but how could he know for sure? He shook his head as he set the kettle to boil again. Stood to reason, if he could recall that his memory was bad, then it couldn't be so bad as all that. It was a little patchy, that was all. No big deal.

He sat at the kitchen table with a fresh cup of tea and picked up the envelope from the Council. It contained details of the home help they were sending to his house. He'd told them he didn't need any help, thank you kindly. Didn't want some do-gooder poking around his kitchen, prying in his fridge, handling things. He could manage just fine.

When the gas main exploded under number 36 flinging slates, bricks and assorted debris high into the night sky, winking across the stars to land in the back gardens and hedges of neighbouring houses, Marvin looked up.

On the heels of the initial boom of the explosion, the low growl and crackle of fire breathed through his open window. He got up from the table, walked towards the window and blinked slowly. Perhaps the street would be back to normal when he opened his eyes, but when he did, he found himself looking straight into the face of the woman across the street. Both her and the baby were staring straight back at him, framed in their window, while fire splashed lurid orange light over the houses.

Lights were going on up and down the street now. People were emerging, bewildered in their nightclothes, stumbling over slippers; drawn towards the fire, they still looked to each other and raised their hands to their mouths, hoping someone else would know what to do. Marvin pulled on his bathrobe and went outside. The crowd milled and clustered, and stepped over the smouldering remnants of exploded house strewn around the street. He was standing at the edge of the crowd when he felt a tug at his sleeve. The baby giggled and tugged again, his chubby hand clasped a handful of Marvin's bathrobe while his mother was busy talking to a woman with long grey braids wearing a Mickey Mouse t-shirt. Marvin held out a finger and the baby grasped and pulled it towards his mouth.

'Hungry are you, buddy?' he asked the baby conspiratorially. 'That what keeps you up at night?' At the sound of his voice, the mother turned her head towards him and narrowed her eyes. 'I always see your light on,' Marvin smiled. She didn't respond. 'Your bedroom light,' he said, wondering again if she spoke English. She raised her eyebrows and drew her baby towards her. 'Not that I'm watching you or anything,' Marvin raised his hands in a gesture of reassurance. 'Nothing like that.' As the woman backed away to the other side of the crowd, he heard the lonely howl of approaching sirens, drawing closer.

The fire engines blasted into the street, a controlled explosion of red paint and blue lights, scattering the residents before them. Firefighters jumped out wearing dayglo jackets and helmets with visors. The police arrived and set about crowd control.

'Move back, please. For your own protection. Stay back.' A kid in uniform herded them across the street, away from the burning building. 'Sorry,' he told them, 'you can't return to your homes just yet but if you'll be patient, we'll let you know as soon as it's safe.'

Finding himself entangled in the docile shuffling of the crowd, Marvin fought his way clear. There must be something he could do to help. Where were the couple that had lived at number 36? Perhaps they were wandering around somewhere dazed and lost, disoriented from the shock, or injured so badly they couldn't move or call out. Someone should be trying to find them. He set off, looking into gardens, around sheds and behind bushes. The cold air poked chill fingers into the folds of his bathrobe and he realised with a familiar dismay that he needed to go, and soon. It was bad enough at his age without the cold, and it sure wasn't helping. He glanced around. He needed to find somewhere quickly.

Marvin edged around a box hedge into a deserted front garden and found a good dark corner. As he stood there, sighing with relief, he looked up at the smoke drifting past the stars. The folks from number 36 had likely been blown up and burnt during the explosion and could even be floating by, within those clouds.

He was just finishing off when he heard a noise behind him. Startled, he spun round and came face to face with a thin, young woman with lank hair, holding a baby. There was something familiar about her. She looked at him and her eyes dropped to his crotch where his hand still flapped and jerked as he attempted to tidy himself back into his pyjama pants.

Her eyes widened in shock for a second then narrowed and her mouth twisted sideways. She pushed a breath out through her nose and turned away. Marvin understood well enough what she meant.

'No. It isn't...I wasn't...It's a tremor...'

Marvin tried to explain but she was already gone. He started to follow and his foot came down on something soft. Oh crap. Please, not dog shit on my slippers, he thought. He looked down and gently lifted his foot.

There on the garden path was a human hand, lying palm up, open, like a strange pale flower in the dark. It had been severed at the wrist but was otherwise intact. By the size of it, and the rings, he could tell it was a woman's hand, must be Mrs 36's. It was her left hand, Marvin noted. He felt a little dizzy as he stood staring at it, wondering what he should do. The ring finger bore an engagement ring and a wedding band, grown slightly too tight over the years and digging into the flesh, the same way Kath's rings had. He remembered the way her hands had lain open on the bedspread, pleading for relief, even as the warmth left her body. And there had been nothing, not one goddamned thing, he could do for her.

Maybe he should pick the hand up but he didn't want to touch it. In any case, he reasoned, you weren't supposed to move a body so probably you shouldn't move pieces of them either. He went to the edge of the garden and looked around, hoping to find someone official nearby, but there was no one. He could see the fire was being brought under control, the flames sinking lower behind the black shadow-puppet silhouettes of his neighbours.

Perhaps he should call for help. He cleared his throat. 'Help?' he tried, but his voice sounded thin and papery. 'Help!' he tried again, but the word jammed in his throat and crushed itself, like it was too big to get out.

As Marvin debated the matter, the hand lay passively on the ground, the fingers curled inwards slightly, lines on the palm picked out by the fading orange light. As he gazed at it, he felt strangely peaceful. Like the scent of some macabre night-blooming flower, the hand released a hypnotic innocence, a frank helplessness that both charmed and troubled him.

Time passed.

The yapping of a dog brought Marvin out of his trance. A small tan-coloured terrier was in the garden, padding eagerly towards the hand. Marvin stepped between the hand and the dog. The dog stopped and looked at Marvin with its head cocked to one side for a second but then continued on, trotting around him towards the hand, its pink tongue poking out over white teeth. Marvin put himself between the two again and, before he thought it all the way through, he growled, low and threatening, and finished with a sharp warning bark and a step forwards. The dog whimpered and backed off out of the garden, then bolted off up the street. Marvin allowed himself a small smile. Not such a helpless old coot after all.

The hand was still there. He'd have to pick it up. That was the only thing to do. He'd pick it up and take it to somebody official and they could deal with it.

The wrist end was seared like a Sunday roast. He bent down and grasped the hand firmly by the wrist. It lolled slightly as he lifted it. It wasn't stiff yet and although it was cool to the touch, it still felt human, real.

He walked to the edge of the path and hesitated. The whole street was outside, including women and children. He couldn't just go wandering around with a severed hand in plain sight. He stepped back into the garden and tried putting it in the pocket of his bathrobe but whichever way he put it in, the other end stuck out and would be clearly visible. Then he had an idea.

Before he could think or change his mind, he tucked the hand inside the elasticated waistband of his pyjama pants, and knotted the cord of his bathrobe tightly over the wrist. He could feel the cool palm and soft fingers resting against the skin of his stomach but it didn't feel bad. The hand was good and secure and wouldn't be upsetting anyone there.

Marvin left the garden and walked back towards the dying fire. All he had to do was find someone in a uniform and explain the situation. Simple.

He was only a few steps away from the crowd when he felt the hand begin to slip. He slowed to a shuffle and tightened the cord on his bathrobe again. But it was too late. Just as he reached the crowd it skidded down further, then stopped. Had things been just a little different, thought Marvin, if a few specific details could've been adjusted, a woman's hand down there would have been welcome.

His shoulders slumped as he looked at the firemen, continuing to pour gallons of water onto the blackened, smoking ruins of number 36. People were bustling about being efficient with clipboards. 'You can go back to your homes now,' a voice announced. 'The gas is off so it's perfectly safe. If you could all clear the area.'

Marvin didn't move. He was worried the hand would slip again, drop down the leg of his pyjama pants and out the other end. The other residents started to drift away in ones and twos, back to their own homes. One of the firemen was looking at Marvin.

'Alright there, mate?' he asked. 'You lost?'

'Um, no, not exactly,' muttered Marvin. He wanted to tell them, but the prospect of fishing the hand from inside his pyjama pants in the middle of the street seemed like a very bad idea.

This wasn't the way he'd imagined things would work out. The ambulance doors slammed and the driver switched the lights off and started the engine. They must have the rest of what was left of the couple from number 36 in there. Perhaps he could run after them, tell them they'd dropped a bit. But before he could form a plan, the ambulance was driving out of the street.

'Are you sure you're okay?' asked the fireman. Marvin nodded, although he wasn't sure, not sure at all. 'You can go home now. Get some rest.' He patted Marvin on the shoulder and moved back to the business of clearing up. Marvin turned and walked, very slowly, back to his house.

Climbing the step to his kitchen door forced him to lift his feet above the low shuffle that had got him this far. The movement dislodged the hand and it skidded down his leg, trailing fingernails down his thigh, fumbling over his kneecap and finally flopping out from the cuff of his pant leg and onto the floor with a slap. He stooped to pick it up, closed the door behind him and gazed around the room. He felt an obligation to the hand now, to protect it and see that it came to no harm. He would figure out what to do later. For now he laid the hand on the bottom shelf of the fridge and closed the door.

He went to the sink, poured a cold cup of tea down the plug hole and set the kettle to boil. This was happening more often lately. It felt like he was forever making tea but hardly ever got to drink any. Through the window, he watched the morning dissolve the remains of the night while the wall clock ticked off another new start.

Marvin sniffed. There was a strong smell of burning. He checked the toaster, the hob and the oven. Sometimes he forgot things so it was best to check. He didn't want to wind up burning the house down. He sat at the table and picked up the letter from the Council, pausing to inspect a red mark on the back of his left hand. It was roughly the shape of India. How had that happened?

There was a banging sound. He listened to it for a while before he realised someone was knocking at his front door. The knocking came again, louder this time. He opened the door. The woman on the doorstep beamed at him, grasped his hand and pumped it up and down.

'You'll be Marvin,' she shouted. And before he could either agree or disagree, she was in his house, bustling down the hall towards the kitchen. 'I'm Judith,' she said, 'the home help? Remember?' She laughed. 'Don't you worry, Marvin, we'll get you sorted out.' She began unpacking a supermarket bag, laying bread, butter, tea and milk out on the worktop. 'I've brought you a few basics. Let's start with a nice cup of tea. Would you like a cup of tea, Marvin?'

How to Not Get Eaten
by Tigers

Jack doesn't look up when the fighting starts. A breeze ruffles the pages of his newspaper and sends the washing on the whirligig spinning. Carol tugs it back around to peg a sock beside its partner. The rusting metal protests with a hoarse squeal. She sighs and goes inside to arbitrate over whose turn it is to choose the cartoon this time, then returns to the garden.

She watches Jack turn a page and give the newspaper a sharp shake, as if telling the stories to stand up straight while he's reading them. Sunlight filters through the garden fence and falls in stripes across his face, which reminds her:

'Molly said a funny thing yesterday.'

There's something about the way Jack doesn't react that makes Carol want to snatch the paper from his hands and throw it over the fence. Instead, she puts her energy into telling him what their daughter said, whether he's listening or not. Despite knowing that the more her words flood out, the more they wash right over him, she can't stop. This is the way they are now. River and rock. She can't be sure exactly when they turned each other into opposing forces.

'She said there's a city where the people all wear masks. Except they wear them on the backs of their heads. Because a tiger won't attack you if it can see you have a face.'

Jack still doesn't look up.

Carol hears herself becoming insistent, the river flowing higher, wilder.

'The tigers come into this city all the time from the surrounding jungles, looking for people to catch and eat. So the clever residents wear masks on the backs of their heads so the tigers won't sneak up on them from behind and devour them when they're walking down the street, going about their daily lives.'

'Where does she get this rubbish from?' Jack scoffs into his newspaper.

The whirligig creaks. Carol doesn't reply, can't get anything past the stone now lodged in her throat. She turns away towards the house, her face hardening, and sees Molly tiptoeing barefoot through sunlight and shade towards them. Her brother is presumably still inside, relishing control of the television. Molly is singing to herself, a song only she knows. Her buttercup dress and her fine blonde hair light up, luminous in each beam of light, and fall back into more subdued tones when she crosses a bar of shadow. As she travels, she appears to flash on and off like a warning signal, a tiny human lighthouse. Look out. Go no further. Steer clear of the rocks.

Carol is mesmerized for a moment simply watching her approach. Her nimble feet on the paving stones, her fingertips trailing through the summer air, her beguiling other-worldly cleverness.

Why doesn't he look up? What can that newspaper possibly contain, what knowledge could he be gaining from it, that could be more urgent than this? Something fierce surges in Carol's chest and she holds her breath, fearful of letting this wildness, this hunger, escape and consume them all. She counts – one tiger, two tiger, three tiger…

Now Jack will look up and see her, really see his daughter, and marvel.

Now.

Now.

Home Security 1

He wants me to know he's been here. The bathroom door is open wide, when I know I closed it before I left. I always keep it closed. There's something distasteful about having the toilet opening off the kitchen. Makes me too aware of my own coiled intestines, like I'm part of the plumbing, a biological conduit for food being processed from one room to the next.

I approach the open doorway and listen hard. No shuffling feet, no surreptitious breathing, only the white-noise whisper of empty space rubbing against cold tiles.

You always said this was temporary. That we'd get somewhere better. I never suspected that your interpretation of 'better' meant you going back to live with your mother. Lucky you had that escape hatch when reality got too real. When I came back that day and found your keys on the table, weighing down a carefully folded sheet of the good writing paper I'd kept for years but seldom found a use for, I knew unfolding and reading the note was superfluous. The words didn't tell me anything the arrangement of paper and keys hadn't told me already.

Gone back to Mum's. Sorry.

That was all. No name. No kisses. No strings attached. Completely free of charge or obligation.

Our love, no matter what that old song says, did not keep us warm. In fact our love entirely failed, over the last long winter, to prevent the gas being cut off, or the rent running overdue.

Through the first mild chills of autumn, you conjured a

certain romance from our lurching from one month to the next, eating our way to the back of cupboards, to the super-noodles and sardines. The more vile and ill-assorted the remnants we fell back on, the greater your delight in serving dinner by candlelight, a dishtowel folded over your arm, a glass jar filled with weeds, charmingly dishevelled, on the kitchen table. It was all a game to you, and I loved you for that. By your rules, it was all a matter of perception. Part of me knew it was all rubbish, no better than a lie, but how seductive it was to believe that all our problems could evaporate if we simply behaved as though they weren't there. In this game, the defining characteristic of a problem was only that it was perceived as such. There were no lies and no truths. In the game of perception, those concepts were meaningless. I was enlightened, raised to a new level of consciousness, and you were my guru. You showed me the way and I followed.

But I still wanted to find another place to live.

Peter Morgan bothered me, with his puffy black leather jacket, his gold link bracelet, sovereign rings and outsized watch.

You thought he was funny.

'Of course he has a key,' you said. 'It's *his* flat after all. He's not going to come in while we're here. He'll just pick up the rent and leave. I'm sure he's got better things to do with his time than perving around his tenants' stuff.'

'But why does he have to come and collect it in cash every month? It's dodgy.'

You grinned and put your arms around me. 'Maybe he's a secret underworld boss running a ring of Romanian begging orphans and trafficking Latvian teenagers into prostitution in his seedy dens of crime and iniquity.'

'That's not funny.'

I thought about Peter Morgan's eyes, that sideways

calculating look he had, the way he never looked at my face.

'You worry too much,' you said, and kissed the top of my head. 'It's not forever.'

Even on my call centre wage, we might've managed if the game of perception had allowed for monthly budgeting but as soon as money came in, you'd burn it off, buying rounds at the union, everyone's best friend. Carpe diem: seize the day and fuck tomorrow.

We celebrated Christmas with a half bottle of whisky and a pack of value mince pies, huddled together, fully dressed under the duvet with only our woolly-hatted heads sticking out, our laughter climbing to the ceiling in clouds. But January was unforgiving and by February, instead of red hearts on Valentine's day, final demands the colour of blood dripped through our letterbox and pooled on the mat.

Believing in you became a physical effort. I had to concentrate so hard it gave me migraines. But I still tried, for you. I wanted to believe.

I still do. I'd give anything to go back to that country where there were no consequences. Now I live in a place with harder edges, where things get left behind, where it hurts.

I miss you.

Of course I miss you.

The game was over for you precisely because it could be. Anything can be a game when you know it's going to end, the board folded up, pieces put back in the box. You took your stuff and more besides, although I can't see why you need half of it back at your mother's. She's probably got spares of everything and another set for 'best'.

Peter Morgan will have noticed your stuff is missing from the bathroom, only one toothbrush and no shaver on the shelf, no stubble coating the basin. Has he gone through the rest of the flat and noted the other evidence of absence? That bleak matrix of order imposed by overlaying my possessions with the empty spaces left by yours.

The possibility of him knowing you're gone makes the fact of him having been here worse. Not just in the flat and in the toilet, but in my life, my head. His thick white fingers prying, his murky glance sliding under the sheets.

I think of you, back at your mum's. Is she tending to your hurts, wrapping you in kindness and unconditional love? I picture you back in your old room, preserved just as it was before you left. Does she knock before she comes in?

The rent money never came from you but Peter Morgan wouldn't know that. Perhaps he suspects today's missing envelope is something to do with the missing person. I wish I'd thought to keep something of you, stashed something away that I could leave casually around the place. Your boots would've been perfect. They were so exclusively you. Only you could wear burgundy velvet Doc Martens, the soft, silly material torn and frayed, the canvas showing underneath.

I should buy a second toothbrush to leave in the bathroom. Maybe some aggressively male toiletries in black and blue packaging. You never went in for any of that but if I'm going to have an imaginary boyfriend, he should have his own personality, don't you think? Perhaps he could also replace some of the other items you found room for in your surprisingly spacious duffle bag.

I keep finding things gone. The alarm clock, all the hand towels, the only sharp knife from the drawer, waking up happy, the pasta strainer, my faith in love. These are all things you took.

And the sex. You took that with you too, and I miss it. Not the soft, cuddly stuff. I could get that from a teddy bear. What I miss is the fucking. The concentrated, sweat-plastered, visceral fucking. The hard stuff. Especially the last weeks, when I'd come home from work and you'd bury yourself inside me before I'd even got my coat off. All the stress and indignity of the day incinerated in the heat of it and we'd emerge, forged securely back together, stronger than anything the world could throw at us. I wonder now what that urgency meant. Were you trying to keep us together or saying goodbye?

You left the red bills, the overdue rent, Peter Morgan and his key, and the Situations Vacant section of the local free paper.

Part-time work, no experience needed, immediate start, excellent earning potential.

I push my misgivings to the back of my mind, along with all the other thoughts I can't afford, and make the call.

Fitting

I was looking for something for the office, something that implied *control* but not *freak*. Not that I believe a pair of shoes can reveal anything about anyone's personality.

To get by, especially at work, I have to play the game, or at least appear to. Mostly I order whatever I need for this charade on the internet, to save the hassle of physically shopping. Unfortunately my feet, although a perfectly standard size five, are difficult to please. They have exaggerated arches and uncooperative bones that provoke chafing and blisters if not suitably housed. I need to do this the old-fashioned way.

Shoe shops used to be full of the scent of leather, and as hushed as a library. I'm not sure when this changed but when I entered *Shoe You* in the Tollgate Centre, it smelled of plastic, sweat, and fake lavender. I squashed my distaste down. I'm not old enough to believe that all the best things are already in the past. Not yet.

I tried on a pair of black courts I suspected of being too high. Trying to move naturally, I took them for a walk over to the mirrors and circled the island of boxy seats. They looked smart enough but made me feel precarious, unbalanced.

'They are so you,' the assistant said, without inflection. Her elaborate eye make-up clashed with her grimy company shirt. The edge of a tattoo poked out from beneath her collar, a slender-tipped butterfly wing in dark cobalt. I checked her expression, hoping for sarcasm but detected only boredom. 'Totally,' she murmured, gazing into the middle distance and taking a nibble from the frayed skin around her thumbnail.

Something felt wrong but it wasn't only the shoes. I stared at the floor and the empty expanse of carpet. My shoes were gone; the shoes I'd walked in wearing, the ones I'd left right there, demurely drawn together next to the seats. Gone.

Apart from the bored assistant, there were few other people in the shop: a man in a suit trying on a pair of fur-lined moccasin slippers, a toddler flailing on the floor while his mother risked a black eye attempting to grip one foot and push a tiny Nike trainer onto it, a woman standing by a full-length mirror on the far side. She looked unremarkable in every way: mid-length brown hair clipped back from her face, nondescript macintosh, black shoulder bag worn with the strap across her body, about my height and build. Just an ordinary everyday person, nothing special. I watched as she turned her back on the mirror to look over one shoulder then the other, twisting her calves this way and that. The shoes she had on were low and practical, a little worn, and unmistakably mine.

At first it seemed funny, if a little awkward. I smiled and hesitated over how best to approach her without causing embarrassment. Surely she must have noticed the shoes weren't new? Perhaps she thought they were made to look that way: distressed, like pre-faded denim. I tried to catch the eye of the assistant but she was talking on the phone behind the counter. I was still dithering, running over possible opening lines in my head, when the woman walked straight out of the shop.

It was the calm way she did it that shocked me initially, left me gaping. I looked around, hoping for a witness, for corroboration, but it seemed nobody else had seen anything. I stood there, blinking in her wake for a couple of seconds before snapping to attention as if someone had shouted my name while I was half asleep. I crossed the threshold of the shop into the main concourse. 'Oi! 'Scuse me!' the assistant yelled, able to see me now I was leaving with goods I hadn't paid for. Half a dozen heads turned in my direction. I kicked the shoes off and continued in my stockinged feet.

Visible through the beige nylon of my tights, my toes were horribly defenceless: likely to be crushed under boots, run over by shopping trolleys, whacked with walking sticks, bitten by dogs. I felt stricken by a sensation I had only experienced in those sweaty, shameful dreams of public exposure. And it wasn't only the physical vulnerability. I realised people were averting their eyes from me, tugging their children closer. I had become someone out of control, possibly dangerous. A crazy shoeless woman.

The thief was almost out of sight, cutting through the crowd with long strides. I pursued her with a kind of skipping run which I hoped minimised the contact my feet had to make with the ground.

I had to catch her before she left the shopping centre. As we neared the sliding doors to the outside world, I saw it was still raining. My embarrassment evaporated, burned off by the rising heat of indignation. But still I didn't shout out. I knew that yelling, combined with my display of shoeless derangement, would only appear even crazier. No one would help and in any case the woman would not stop. I had enough money to let her go, turn back, and buy a replacement pair of shoes, but my sense of outrage pushed me forwards.

The paved pathway around the side of the shopping centre was sheltered and dry but when she moved off across the car park, I paused. This was the point where I should turn back, I knew, but again dismissed the possibility. The wet pavement felt coldly intimate against my unprotected soles. The feet of my tights blackened as dirty water crept between my toes but by this stage nothing could have stopped me.

I quickened my pace as she crossed the road but gained no ground on her. We continued, separate but together, joined by an invisible cord that neither lengthened nor shortened. I tried to picture her face, thinking that if I could remember what she looked like I would somehow understand her motives. But where her features should have been there was only a vague impression of a face – whatever it was that made her *her* was impossible to bring to mind. Whenever I came close, my recollection veered away as if repelled by an opposing magnetic charge.

I broke into a slow jog and she did the same. Without looking around she maintained the distance between us. The rain grew heavier, driving down in diagonal sheets. My fringe stuck in clumps to my forehead. I increased my pace and so did she. The race didn't last long; I was out of shape. I stopped, pressed the heel of my hand into the stitch below my ribs, and sucked in air. The woman took advantage of the break to remove an umbrella from her handbag and put it up. I pushed the hair from my eyes and watched. She was toying with me. I started walking again and she set off too. We kept a slower pace this time. We walked, and we walked.

At some point the rain stopped and she folded her umbrella away. The sun came out, high and blind in a washed-out sky. We were passing through streets I no longer recognised, threading through the fringes of the city. The streets were hushed and an air of expectation hung over the houses. The glass in their windows flashed and glittered. There were no other pedestrians but even if there had been, I knew I couldn't ask for help. The woman looked as composed and unremarkable as she had in the shop, whereas I was unkempt and sweating in my damp overcoat. Hoisting my bag over my shoulder, I removed it and slung it over my arm.

I lost track of how long we had been walking. It felt like

hours, days. I should've turned back. I wasn't especially attached to the shoes but it was no longer about them. I wanted to know why she had done it, why she was still doing it, but the distance between us remained. She was always just on the edge of disappearing from view. The sun grew hot and warmed the tarmac, releasing a heavy, oily smell. The soles of my tights wore right through, rolled up over my feet and encircled my ankles in ragged, bloody frills. I imagined the skin on the soles of my feet doing the same, the skin rupturing, peeling up and away from the flesh, leaving my feet a splayed mass of contracting muscle and bones. I pictured reaching down, grabbing hold of the loose flaps of skin at the ankle and pulling, rolling the skin up off the flesh of my legs, the thin connective tissue between skin and sinew like damp spider webs. In my imagination, I crossed my arms over and bunched the empty skin in my hands and tugged it up over my hips, like taking off a dress. I eased it over my shoulders and extracted my arms, my hands, each finger popping out as if released from a tight-fitting glove, leaving the complete skin draped around my neck in a heavy cowl. Finally, I dragged it over my head and dropped the whole lot in the gutter.

This scenario, this process, repeated over and over in my mind as I walked. It kept me going. There was comfort in the repetition and, with each reimagining, I refined the details: the delicate unfurling of the complicated areas between my legs, over my chest, around my mouth, the skin coming away in one unbroken piece. The satisfaction of that, like a single ribbon of apple peel. It began to seem real. I felt lighter, cleaner. The air on my exposed veins and blood vessels was cool and alive with something like electricity. I was pared down to my essentials, all branding removed. I was purely human.

How much better it would be. Better than any self-knowledge, to lose all concept, all memory of self, to lay that burden down, absolved of the responsibility. Here was an end to existence that was not death but a new kind of life. Life as a harmonious expression of a larger cosmic force that didn't care about packaging.

And simply to keep walking, keep going, one step after another, feeling no pain. I glanced over my shoulder at the trail of footprints now drying to a dusky russet on the tarmac. They looked so old they reminded me of cave paintings and that idea seemed entirely fitting. If the first signs of individuality were hand prints, then it made sense that these footprints should mark my departure from identity; my exit from the stage of me.

We came to a bridge over a slow-moving river. The woman stopped on the far side. This could have been my opportunity to catch up and confront her. But now it no longer mattered. What need did I have for her, or what she had taken from me? I fixed my eyes on the horizon and let it draw me on, turning the world under my naked feet as I walked, rolling it gently from heel to toe. By the time I crossed the bridge and reached the place where she had stood, she was no more than a reflection dispersing in the water below.

Loving the Alien

I don't know about you, but I've never bought into all this 'Men Are From Mars and Women Are From Venus' malarkey.

For a start, I know for a fact that Derek is from Bathgate. And considering Venus has a surface temperature hot enough to melt lead and an atmosphere filled with clouds of sulphuric acid, it's not somewhere I'm particularly keen to visit, even for a day trip.

Of course we have our differences – me and Derek. Otherwise it'd be creepy. But despite them, we'd been getting along great, until recently. After last night's little scene I honestly think it's time for me to pack my bags and move on.

'Please,' he said. 'Please, Sandra, pleeeease…' He was making those little praying hands at me. Good grief. Now, I like to see a man beg as much as the next woman, but Derek was beginning to get on my nerves.

'No,' I told him flat. 'You know that green body paint brings me out in a rash.'

But he kept on wheedling.

I tried to bargain with him. 'Look, sweetheart,' I said, 'you can still be my James T Kirk. I'll even let you teach me what love is – again. I just don't want to be green anymore.'

You wouldn't know it to look at Derek. He kept it well hidden, I can tell you. We'd been seeing each other for a few months before it came up. We'd been having a night in, pizza in front of the telly, bottle of wine, all nice and cosy, when a trailer came on for the new Star Trek film. He asked me if I'd like to see it and I told him sure, I'd love to. Then he asked, all casual, if I like Star Trek and I said 'Yeah, it's cool. Beam me up, Scotty!' Thinking nothing of it.

But when I looked round, Derek had this big, daft, open-mouthed grin on his face, like a cartoon puppy looking at a juicy bone. He grabbed my hand and stared, all intense, into my eyes. 'From the moment we met,' he said, 'I knew you weren't like other women.'

Well, he got that right. But I couldn't help thinking that Derek's delight suggested a failure to appreciate the nature of individuality. There is no being in this whole entire universe exactly like me, but then no matter how long or how carefully you look, you'll never find another Derek either, or another you. We are all cosmically different, each of us a very specific and unrepeatable collection of atoms, with our own very specific and unrepeatable hopes, fears, dreams, hang-ups, screw-ups and longings. And while that makes us all unique and separate, it also gives us something in common and brings us together.

It wasn't the time to point this out though. 'Oh Sandra, where have you been all my life?' he gushed. He was fair transported, so he was.

'It's just a film, Derek,' I told him. 'Don't get your jollies in a knot.'

Well, after that he started taking any opportunity he could to slip a bit of Trekkie talk into the conversation. One night in bed he started making all these weird noises. Kind of grunting and choking. I was about to perform the Heimlich manoeuvre when he stopped and looked at me and said, 'So you don't speak Klingon then?'

It was right about then I should've left.

But you don't see what's happening. It's all just a series of episodes and you don't see the big picture till much later. I wasn't bothered about the dressing up at first. It was just a bit of harmless fun. We all have our little quirks after all. And it certainly seemed to push Derek's buttons. Improved his stamina no end. So I reckoned wearing a pair of sparkly deeley-boppers and some blue lipstick was a small price to pay.

But after a while, when it got to the stage that I was dressing up every single time, I did start to feel a little... overlooked. Derek didn't seem to want me anymore, just me, myself. It was as if I wasn't different enough for him anymore. Don't get me wrong, I'm not some hopeless romantic, I do know that in every relationship, that initial hot flash of infatuation has to transform into something more stable over time. But if you're lucky it sets, like a molten planet cooling, into a world you both want to settle on and share, maybe even colonise, with its high mountains, lush valleys and deep, rolling oceans. Ideally, you'll want to preserve a scattering of exotic undiscovered regions just to provide a few surprises along the way. That's what love between two people is: your own Home World. That's what I'd always been looking for, what I had hoped I'd finally found with Derek. But rather than allowing our planet to form, Derek grew increasingly distracted by certain design features.

He became more ambitious, his set-ups more elaborate. The ears became a bit of an issue. It wasn't enough that Mr Spock got to experience emotion for the first time. He needed perfect ears for the occasion, and Derek would spend ages sitting at the kitchen table carving them out of potatoes before he'd come up to bed. Eventually I got tired of waiting.

His fixation with the green Rigelian dancing girl was really just the last straw. Our relationship's final frontier.

It's 3am when I shoulder my bag and tiptoe from the bedroom. No point in waking Derek and risking a scene. I navigate the darkened hallway using only the faint glow from the tip of my extended index finger. Derek's face would be some picture if he could see this.

Outside, the stars are spread out across the sky, at once both lonely and welcoming. I press the button on my key and the wheels of the Honda Civic parked at the kerb rise and disappear smoothly into its elongating chassis. My starship hovers there, waiting for me.

I'm not too sure where I'm going, where I might one day find somewhere, or someone, I can call home.

Her Feelings About Auckland

'I wish you wouldn't do that,' she says. 'You're always trying to put things in boxes.'

He pauses and looks up from the box of junk he's sorting through. Rain patters on the attic skylight, a peaceful backing track to his rapid rewind through their conversation. He'd like to pinpoint the problem with the boxes before responding. He recalls talking about how pointless it was to keep all this broken stuff in the attic, but nothing that provides a clue to her current irritation.

'Um…?'

She knows he's pretending to be clueless so he doesn't have to engage with what she's saying. 'You know. That thing you do. Compartmentalising everything?'

He shakes his head. 'I thought we agreed we were going to have a proper clear-out? We don't need any of this stuff.'

They both go back to raking through old lamps and burst tennis rackets.

'It's not just stuff though. There are memories and associations, *feelings* attached to everything. It's not healthy, this ability of yours to turn all that off whenever it doesn't suit you.'

He sighs and stares into the mouth of the old toaster before dropping it back into the box. 'I'd like to get this finished today.'

'We will. But we don't need to be like robots about it. People, *normal* people, don't work that way. You can't separate thinking from feeling.'

'Course I can. Some thoughts are just thoughts. You don't have to get all worked up about everything. All emotional when there's no need.'

'I'm not getting worked up,' she says, her voice rising. 'I'm just saying it's not possible to think *anything* without having some form of emotional response to it.'

'I'd say it is.'

'And I'd say you're wrong. Every thought you have, no matter how mundane, you also have a feeling about it. I'll give you an example.' She sets down the tatty box file she was holding, puts her hands on her hips and looks above his head for inspiration. 'Auckland is the capital of New Zealand. There.'

He scratches his head. 'I think it's Wellington, actually.'

'That's not the point.'

'It isn't?'

'No. The point is, I don't know what the capital of New Zealand is, and crucially, I don't care. No offence to the people of New Zealand, or the residents of Auckland—'

'Wellington.'

'Whatever. Auckland's status as a city really doesn't concern me at all.'

'Fair enough. I don't think they'd be too bothered what you think either.'

'But then, the more I think about Auckland, I start to wonder about other things. Like why's it called Auckland? Does it have Auks? What is an Auk anyway?' She punctuates each question with upraised palms, a little higher each time. 'Do they still exist or are they extinct? Is that the fault of human settlers? Did they arrive, see all the Auks and decide to name the place after them, then kill them all, without really meaning to, but in the way things get killed when you're not paying attention, not making sure they're safe. And then they're left living in this Land of the Auk with no Auks in it anymore. That must make them feel sad and a bit bad about themselves, or their ancestors. And also, isn't there's something called a Great Auk. I mean, are they really that great?'

He looks at her standing there with her hands raised above her head, breathless and indignant. 'What? *What* are you on about?'

'The thing is,' she plunges on, aware she's maybe overdone the Auk thing but still hopeful it'll all pan out, 'before I know it, I'm having a whole bunch of feelings about Auckland after all.' Her eyes feel hot and there's a tightness inside her throat. She knows she's close to becoming ridiculous but feels precariously self-righteous. 'Those poor trusting Auks, what chance did they have? With their big stupid-looking beaks and useless stubby wings.'

'Is that not a Dodo?' He smiles, hoping she'll join in.

She swallows, blinks twice in quick succession and looks at the skylight. 'I am trying here! I'm trying to explain how I feel.'

'About Auckland?'

'…'

The rain fizzles against the skylight, like a dying firework.

Bingo Wings

'Bar doesn't open till six, love. You may as well have a seat.' The barmaid with the yellow hair was blunt but not unfriendly.

'That's okay, I'll just wait here, thanks.' Dora knew, as soon as the shutters clattered up and crashed out of sight, there'd be a stampede for the bar. Some of these old dears might look sweet but they'd elbow you right in the tits to get in front.

She shifted her weight from one foot to the other in her queue of one and wondered about the mice. Everyone knew fine the place was infested. She didn't mind sharing, as long as the cheeky wee bastards stayed out of sight till the bingo was finished.

'Come on, ladies. Time you opened up. You've a customer waiting.' Colin sidled up to Dora. He was a little ferret of a man with spots on the back of his neck that glistened under the lights like boiled sweets. 'Got all your books, Doreen? I think you might get lucky tonight!' He nudged Dora theatrically in the ribs and winked. 'I have Caller's Intuition.'

'Oh aye?' Dora raised her eyebrows at him. 'Better make sure and call my numbers then.'

'For you, gorgeous? Anything.'

She was more than twice his age. It wasn't as if she minded that fact, but pretending like she was still a young thing? Some of the other old biddies loved it though, got all giggly and excited. She busied herself rummaging in her handbag. Colin went off to look for a more receptive audience and the shutters rattled up.

Up in the balcony, the usual crew were installed at their table. Dora laid down the tray with their order of drinks and crisps.

'Nice one, Dora,' said Jim, taking a deep pull on his pint and sitting back in his chair. He'd get himself a sly whisky at the bar later when it was his round and Mary would pretend to be none the wiser. Mary and Jim were good at being married. They had a natural ability, the way some folk were good at singing or dancing. It was a gift. The way they accommodated each other reminded Dora of a kind of old-fashioned waltz, each of them anticipating the other's moves. There was a grace about them that couldn't be hidden by any amount of brown cardigans or puffy ankles.

Alec was there too. Mary and Jim's grown-up son wasn't quite all there in the head. Poor soul. His lips were always wet and his clothes, although clean, looked like they'd been corkscrewed onto his body. Sometimes he would get agitated and start shouting and Mary had to miss her game to take him out of the hall until he calmed down. A lot of folk tutted at her for even bringing him. But what was she supposed to do? He might be a grown man, but she couldn't leave him on his own at home.

Dora handed Alec his lemonade and watched as he settled to sucking on his straw, eyes slightly out of focus, completely contented, like a baby with a bottle.

'Has she phoned then?' asked Mary, through a mouthful of cheese & onion crisps.

'No, not this week. She'll be busy. The time difference, and her working shifts, it's hard for her to find a good time. Doesn't want to wake me up in the wee hours just for a chat.' Angela was a nurse and worked hard at it. She'd always been a caring girl, always wanted to help others. Dora pictured her cycling to work in the Australian sunshine, barbecuing dinner on the beach, poised on a surfboard at the crest of a wave, her black hair streaming out behind her like a banner. No wonder she didn't have time to phone. Dora understood. Like the song said, if you loved someone, set them free.

She poured half of her bottle of stout into a glass, arranged her books on the table and tested her dabber on a scrap of paper, making a trail of red dots.

The first games of the night passed without so much as a line for any of them. Dora waved away Jim's protestations that it was his round and hurried back down to the bar, eager to beat the break-time rush. She felt restless this evening and wanted to be doing something. She passed Jim in the press of the crowd streaming down the stairs on her way back up, no doubt using a pretend trip to the toilet as cover for his quick whisky. At the table, Mary was trying to pacify Alec who'd got himself in a bit of a state. He was hunched over, making a mournful keening sound that made something clench and twist in Dora's chest.

'I'll just take him for a walk around the bandits,' said Mary. She chivvied Alec, who was a good foot taller than her, out from his seat and led him by the elbow towards the stairs.

Dora sat on her own and looked out over what had once been a dance floor, back before everyone had televisions and computers to keep them busy. There had been a revolving stage on a massive turntable at the far end. When one band finished their set, the whole thing would revolve, and a fresh band would strike up the next number as they swung into view. Non-stop dancing. That was the Palais' claim to fame and a lot of folk took to it like it was an order, staying on the floor for hours, sweating and spinning till they couldn't walk or think in a straight line.

The polished boards were now covered by a greasy carpet with a geometric design, the space filled with rows of

Formica tables and chairs, all kept in their place by thick metal bolts through the legs into the floor. Near the ceiling, the old chandeliers and mirror balls that used to spill a confetti of light over the dancers below, had been replaced with blank white globes, like dead planets. Life had moved on.

The memories this place sprung on her at times disconnected her from the here and now, as if time itself was some kind of puzzle she'd never be able to solve without going mad. All the same, being at the bingo was still better than sitting at home, waiting for nothing to happen. It always did. Then that nothing would become a something – an emptiness that pressed in on her, making her heart race and her hands shake. That was when the other, darker thoughts would creep out of the corners and torment her with detail.

The lights dimmed as Colin again climbed the steps to the caller's raised podium. The chatter died down. People coughed and shifted their feet in nervy anticipation.

Saturday nights were serious money, the sort of money that could change a person's life, if you wanted it changing. Their club linked up with a dozen others across the country and all the prize money was pooled, so your chances of success were much lower but if you did win, the jackpot was far bigger than on an ordinary night. Enough to take a good long holiday in Australia, as Mary had pointed out more than once. Like Dora hadn't worked that out for herself.

The silence stretched tight as all heads turned towards the podium. Colin was obviously savouring his moment as everyone hung on the very edge of his silence. He delivered his line with gravity. 'Eyes down for the National Game.'

The electronic board mounted on the wall at the far end of the hall lit up in a simulated star burst which dissolved to reveal a grid within which the lucky numbers would be illuminated as they were called.

'Sixteen. One and six, sixteen.'

She scanned her card for the number. *Never Been Kissed.* Colin was under orders from club HQ not to use the lingo. More games could be played each session without the frills. But Dora remembered them all, whether she wanted to or not.

She remembered walking into the Palais de Danse on her sixteenth birthday. Like stepping inside a giant hollowed-out wedding cake at Christmas – all creamy columns and layered balconies decorated with pink and white mouldings, the edges trimmed with lights.

Charlie only had a couple of years on her but seemed much older. His swaggering walk, Italian suit, the hank of black hair, heavy with Brylcreem. She knew he got into the fights that broke out in the dark recesses under the balconies where a dangerous current of young men circled like sharks. He would have cuts on his knuckles, maybe a graze on his face, a hint of swelling around his mouth. Somehow this only made his gentleness with her more overpowering. She'd been such an eejit. Never been kissed, right enough. When he dipped his head down to her and spoke softly, rested his hands on her waist, she'd felt a fierce desire to be a damn sight more than kissed. If this was love, it wasn't about hearts or flowers. It was all hot breath and sinew and need.

'Seven and eight, seventy eight.' *Heaven's Gate.*

She'd gone outside for some air. Really she was looking for Charlie.

Outside, the front of the Palais was a large rectangular slab of art deco with thin leaded windows and a triangular gable over four columns. Behind the façade, the hunched barn of the main hall squatted like a shameful secret.

'Dora! Over here.' He was leaning against the side of the building, smoking. His face flared in the glow from the burning tip of his cigarette before falling back into darkness. 'Come on, I've got something to show you.'

Around the back of the building, among the empty crates and rubbish bins, they slid together into a darkened doorway marked Deliveries Only. A hand at the small of her back pulled her in close, another slid under her full skirts. There was a small thud as the back of her head bumped against the metal door.

'Four and one. Forty-one.' *Life's begun.*

Back inside, as they slow danced, her head on his shoulder, breathing in his smell, her limbs seemed not to be joined to her body in the same way. The springs under the dance floor no longer supported her as she moved but seemed to work against her, causing her to lurch and sway, to cling to Charlie. Thinking of the potential consequences made her feel queasy. But everyone knew the first time was safe. They'd be more careful in future.

'Two and eight. Twenty-eight.' *In a state.*

The pain was more than anyone could ever have warned her. It rose up in dark red waves that swamped her completely. 'Pain' was too small and weak a word for this force. It was bigger than her, bigger than the room, the hospital, something separate and unstoppable. Her mother walked over to the window in small precise steps and stared into the darkness with her lips pressed together.

The numbers kept coming and Dora stamped them off one after

another. She glanced up at the podium. Soon the game would be over and Colin would be reduced once more to making smutty innuendoes to get attention. He would stay up there all the time if they'd let him, Dora thought.

Her card was filling up as if Colin was reading the numbers over her shoulder. She felt sweat prickle on the back of her neck. Her sense of being on the edge of something increased. She pressed her forearms down hard on the table, trying to get a grip without making it obvious she needed to. It felt as if the whole balcony was tipping forwards into the hall in the direction of the café at the far end, where the revolving stage used to be.

The whole affair had been managed by two hand cranks, one on either side of the stage. 'Watch this,' Charlie had whispered in her ear, then walked that walk of his towards the stage. Dora watched as he and three of his pals took hold of the cranks, two men to each, and started working them as hard as they could. The stage began to turn, slowly at first, then with increasing speed as the Johnny Kildare Orchestra went into the closing bars of 'I'll be Loving You Always'. The band leaned in against the spin, tried their best to look as if nothing was happening, and kept playing. They were half way round when there was a grinding noise and the stage left its runners altogether, tipping the band off into a flailing pile of tuxedoes and instruments. Cheers went up from the crowd. Charlie and his mates sped past, an irate brass section close behind.

'One and three. Thirteen.' *Unlucky for some.*

There was no reason to think Angela *wasn't* nursing in Australia. No reason at all. Certainly no reason to imagine she'd ended up a druggie, like those lassies in the flats, shacked up with some arsehole who beat her up, or with ten kids she couldn't feed that got taken off her one by one by the social, or giving hand-jobs to men who avoided eye contact and swore at her when they came, or beaten and dumped in a ditch with her own bra twisted around her neck, eyes wide open, staring at the sky for days, weeks, without anybody noticing she was gone. And all of it made possible because she believed her own mother didn't want her, had never loved her. But that wasn't true at all.

What was true and what wasn't didn't make much difference to what happened to a person in life. It hadn't to her, or to Angela – if that was even her name now, wherever she was, whoever she was. Adoption was easily done in those days. Happened all the time – the product of ignorance and prejudice. She wasn't anything special. She just thought too much. That'd always been her problem. Left to her own devices, her mind invariably wandered back to the well-worn track of whatever happened to her girl. Hoping everything worked out for her, hoping she had a good life, hoping she didn't think too badly of her. Hope was a bastard, but it was also the only thing she had that couldn't be taken off her. It was both her escape and her prison; life support and life sentence. It pulled her through the years, days, seconds, gifting and cursing her from breath to breath with a string of empty promises. Without it she'd hardly be human.

There was a sudden eruption of activity right at the back of the balcony. A woman with wispy white hair and enormous glasses shouted and leapt out of her seat, squawking and flapping.

'We have a claim!' announced Colin.

A uniformed girl came running to check the woman's card, the microphone buzzing in her hand.

'I need to see your card.'

'But I've not won!' shouted the woman who by now looked as if she was about to take off. 'Look – there!' She pointed towards the shadows in the corner behind her seat. 'Mouse, you stupid girl! Not house – *mouse*! See? Over there by the wall. Bold as brass, looking at me like it owns the bloody place.'

Dora stood and peered in the direction the woman was pointing and, right enough, there sat a small brown mouse, perfectly still, its black eyes glinting. Calmly, as if pleased it had made its point, it turned and padded out of sight.

The hall was in an uproar, some were laughing, some shouting abuse at the woman for interrupting the game. Colin kept repeating, 'Can I have the code number please?'

Eventually the girl shouted over her mic, 'No claim!' and the game continued.

'Three and one. Thirty one.' *Get up and run.*

Full house. Couldn't be. But it was.

Alec was watching her, a droplet of spit slowly descending from his lower lip. Without looking up from her game, Mary reached over with a tissue and wiped it away before tucking the tissue into the sleeve of her cardigan.

Dora felt a falling, draining sensation that left the top of her head buzzing with cold, her ears filled with sea-shell emptiness. This wasn't supposed to happen to her. She looked at Mary and Jim, at the rows of heads in the hall below, bowed over their cards.

Then the realisation. She didn't have to say a thing. If she simply waited, someone else's card would fill up. Just a matter of time. All she needed to do was wait.

Colin's intercom crackled into life carrying the distant shouts of a winning claim in one of the other halls. Dora twisted her card tight and pushed it firmly into the neck of her almost empty bottle.

Mary and Jim were comparing their missed numbers, groaning and laughing over their near misses. Mary looked up at her, 'No luck either then, Dora?'

Dora felt light, as if she could launch herself off the balcony and fly in great swooping arcs around the hall. 'No, not tonight, Mary. Maybe next time.'

'We live in hope eh?' said Jim, rising from his seat and gathering up the empty glasses. 'Same again?'

Home Security 2

The interview was in a second floor flat converted into offices. The conversion amounted to no more than stripping out anything homey and throwing in a few desks, swivel chairs and ring binders. The air smelled of sweat and adolescent aftershave. Crooked venetian blinds were drawn against the sunlight, casting the room into shadow save for the glow from a PC screen. The bluish light made everyone in the room look like corpses, including Derek and his business partner, Darren, both of whom wore wide ties and grimy-looking pastel shirts.

Derek looked me up and down and offered me his hand to shake, already bored with the formalities. He glanced at the single printed page of my CV, sighed and tossed it onto the desk. My earlier misgivings started muttering and edging forward in my mind but I herded them back and shushed them into silence.

'Take a seat over there. Be with you in a minute.'

There were four of us, lined up against the wall on orange plastic chairs. Two youngish guys and a middle-aged woman. The faint whiff of desperation hung around us like an eggy fart. I fixed my attention on the thin ribbon of blue sky showing through a gap in the blinds and silently repeated the mantra 'good earning potential good earning potential'. Derek and Darren bustled about, letting off volleys of forced laughter and shuffling bundles of fliers and clipboards, attaching pens on short lengths of string. We waited, not looking at each other.

'Right, we've got two teams today,' Derek announced, handing out the clipboards. His shirt buttons strained over his stomach as he inflated his already bulky torso with enough enthusiasm to achieve take-off velocity.

The red plastic covering on my clipboard was split at the corners, the hardboard showing through.

'Margaret and David, you're with Darren.'

The older woman and one of the young guys looked at Darren who winked back and made a clicking noise with his tongue against the roof of his mouth. Neither of them appeared reassured by this.

'Kirsty and John, you're with me.'

'Joe,' said the guy sitting next to me. 'My name's Joe.' His voice lacked conviction, like he didn't care all that much, would be willing to be John, or James, or even Janet as long as he got paid at the end of the day. There were dark circles under his eyes and his chin looked raw and patchy as if he'd shaved in a hurry.

Derek blinked and scribbled something on his own clipboard. 'If you say so.'

'What you've got to remember, what you've got to impress upon the homeowner, is that you're not selling anything.'

'We're not?'

I glanced over at Joe. He raised his eyebrows and gave a small apologetic shrug. This was the closest we'd come to communicating since we met five minutes earlier. Crammed together into the back seat of Derek's Corsa as it pushed through traffic, it was too much too soon. Joe cleared his throat and I sat on my hands. We both stared at the back of Derek's head.

'No, you're not. No selling at all. You're giving them information. No strings attached. Completely free of charge or obligation.' Derek's voice sounded like a pre-recorded message playing from somewhere at the back of his throat. While the words came out level, he was swerving around a builder's van parked in the bus lane and giving the finger to the driver behind. 'The only cost to them is a minute of their time to allow you to deliver that information.'

Derek was taking us for an aptitude test.

'No quicker way to find out if you can do this job than going out and doing it. I don't have time to waste fannying around, training you up on the off-chance, only to get out in the field and find you can't cut it.'

Joe scratched his nose and leant forward. 'But if we're not selling, then what—'

'You're wondering what's in it for us? Where's the payoff?'

'Well, yes. I suppose I am,' said Joe, turning his head as we passed a police car parked with blue lights flashing outside a locksmith's shop. 'Wondering.'

'What you're after, the prize you seek, the Holy Grail of your quest, and the only way you're going to be leaving with any cash in your pocket today, by the way, is... the *Referral*.' Derek rolled the word out like an expensive rug for us to admire.

We appreciated the word silently, and after a suitable pause Derek continued.

'Your job is to deliver the information. And then – pay attention both of you, this is the important bit – then, persuade them to sign up for a free Home Security Consultation.'

Joe nodded. 'And that'll be the sales guys?'

'Specialists,' replied Derek, his neck stiffening. 'Home security specialists.'

Joe looked over at me, rolled his eyes and smiled.

'And those specialists just happen to sell security systems?' I said, returning the smile, the ice broken. We could be allies, me and Joe, I thought – help each other through this, have a bit of a laugh. He'd have his reasons for being here, same as I had mine.

'Hahaha!' Derek laughed like a machine jamming. 'You're a sharp one, Kirsty, aren't you? Sharp as a tack. I could tell straight off. I reckon you could be one of my top earners.'

Joe turned away to look out of his side window, our conspiracy disbanded before it was properly formed.

'You need to focus on your goal. The Referral. That's all you're after. Never mind what comes next. Specialists. Sales guys. Whatever. Just keep your eyes on the prize. You are not sales people. At no point in your pitch will you mention the word sales. You will no more say sales to the homeowner than you would say *tit-wank*.'

An intake of breath from Joe. I sighed inwardly but didn't react, just kept staring at the back of Derek's head, the way his neck bulged over his off-white collar, the rigidity of his gelled hair. I stifled a yawn. This was going to be a long afternoon.

Derek took a corner fast. I grabbed the door handle to keep from falling into Joe's lap.

'If, and only if, the homeowner wishes to act upon the recommendations made in the consultation then our specialist will make some suitable suggestions from the product range carried by Apex Security. But that's not your concern. Your concern is...?'

'The referral,' Joe and I parroted simultaneously without enthusiasm.

'That's right! Top marks. And what word do you not use?'

I decided to let Joe have that one, by way of a peace offering.

'Sales,' he said.

'Right again! Gold star!'

'Or tit-wank,' Joe added with a snigger and a sidelong glance in my direction.

I stared out at the traffic as if I hadn't heard him. Responding to this kind of crap only makes it more important. Some guys think any sexual reference is like Kryptonite to women. I don't get it. And I don't care enough about what they think to be arsed putting them right.

'Yes. Good.' Derek stopped at a set of lights and rolled his shoulders. 'This isn't rocket science. All you need to do is follow the steps.'

The lights started to change. Derek was half way across the junction before they reached green.

'Fire away,' said Joe, rubbing his hands together, all matey now.

'First impressions. Smile.' Derek swivelled his head round while changing gear and demonstrated by stretching his lips over his teeth. He turned back and jerked the steering wheel, barely missing a cyclist.

'Tell them you're sorry to disturb them. Tell them you represent Apex Home Security Systems. Tell them we have representatives in their area this week and are offering homeowners a free, no obligation Home Security Consultation. Now, this is the first point of potential disconnect. Unless you're very lucky, they'll be trying to close the door about now, thinking about their dinner going cold on the table. Do not let them close that door. Keep talking. Maintain eye contact. Don't even fucking blink. Got that?'

Derek looked at us from his rear view mirror, not blinking.

We both nodded mutely.

'I gave you four distinct points in the process there. Can either of you tell me what they were?'

I'd given up trying to be friendly so jumped in before Joe could open his mouth.

'Smile. Apologise. Give them the pitch. Don't fucking blink.'

'Perfect! See? Knew you were a sharp one.'

Derek reeled off more points in the process but they all came down to getting folk to sign a form agreeing to a home visit. The pre-recording of his voice continued to play from somewhere behind his tongue but it seemed to be at a lower volume. Now I knew what was expected, all I wanted was to get it over with.

The tall flats and shop fronts eventually gave way to gardens and houses with driveways. It was all so clean. Even the leaves on the trees looked like they'd just come out the wash and been hung up on the branches to dry in the sunshine.

'Here we are,' said Derek. He rolled his window down and lit a cigarette.

I rolled mine down too. The only sound was the rustling of leaves and the distant laughter of unseen children.

'Prime customer base,' said Derek, flicking ash out of the window. 'Folk here have nice stuff. They don't want some druggy little scrote from the council estate swiping the kiddies' iPods or their Blu-ray player. But the number one thing they want to preserve is their *feeling* of security. It's not about the stuff. It's the violation, the loss of peace of mind. *It's not what they take, it's what they leave behind.* Let them know you understand that.

'If a man answers the door, use words like *protection* and *defence*. Ask them if they work away from home a lot. If it's a woman, use words like *attack* and *invasion*. If they have a big dog, point out that dogs can be poisoned. Make them feel vulnerable and they'll be thankful you're there to help.

'Joseph, you start at that end, take the even numbers. Kirsty, you take the odds and start at the other end. We'll rendezvous here in half an hour. Now off you go and get me those referrals.'

The wind hissed through the hedges, following me as I walked the length of the street. Sunlight reflected flatly from double-glazed windows. From the first house I approached, I heard a television playing and voices, laughter, family noises. Already I felt self-conscious. At least I could do the apologising part with sincerity. I pulled my shoulders back a notch, hung a smile on my face and rang the doorbell. The door swung open, fanning rich cooking smells over me. My empty stomach growled.

A teenage boy wearing a Radiohead T-shirt, fringe covering most of his face, took one look at my smile-and-clipboard combo and retreated along the hall. When he got to the stairs he cocked his head and shouted 'Muhuuh, s'feyoo,' before shuffling out of sight.

The door started to swing shut. I put out a hand to stop it slamming but it was caught from inside by a woman who raised her eyebrows at my still-outstretched hand.

'Yes? Can I *help* you?' The pointed way she emphasised *help* made it clear that what she actually had in mind was something closer to *punch*. She pulled the door back and held on to it.

I did my best to keep my smile in place and launched into the spiel. She nodded impatiently so I cut to the chase, gave her the stuff about being in the area, blah blah. I raced through it, wanting it to be over. I tried to maintain eye contact, like Derek said, but couldn't stop my gaze falling. As soon as she got the gist, she deployed a brisk 'sorrythanksbutnothanks' and closed the door with a thump.

I continued to fail my way up the street, becoming more abject the further I got until I was knocking on doors only to apologise before slinking back off down the drive. I couldn't do it. What right did I have to introduce fear into these people's lives? I decided I'd finish the rest of the street, but whether I got a referral or not, I wouldn't be doing this again. I'd find another way to make the rent.

Then there was this one house.

It was the last one on the street and the door was open, just a crack. I knocked and it swung inwards until the handle bumped on the inside wall, leaving the house wide open. I couldn't leave it like that so I stepped inside, balancing on one foot, trying to grab the handle without setting my other foot down. That way I wasn't really inside, wasn't crossing their threshold, not all of me. But then, without knowing quite how it happened, I was.

'Hello?' I called out, but the house was quiet. Not a dead silence, more tranquil than empty. I continued along the hall: solid wood floors, a gilt-framed mirror, a shoe rack crammed with a jumble of trainers and boots. My heels sank into the soft pile of the patterned rug. I called again, projecting my voice up the stairs. 'Hello-oh? Anyone home?' I'd already decided that I wouldn't attempt to deliver my pitch although, in some ways, it was a tailor-made opportunity to demonstrate the benefits of greater home security. I could've been anyone.

Still no answer.

I peered into the first room. Comfy looking sofas, walls lined with bookshelves, an upright piano in the corner. Two empty wine glasses together on the coffee table, dregs pooled into red dots.

There were photographs, professional studio shots of a couple and one child, a little boy, posed on an entirely white background, a safe well-lit place where nothing but their happiness could exist and no other realities could intrude.

I looked at the spines of the books. Mostly fiction, some good stuff, some trash, bulky hardbacks on architecture and gardening. A ladies' watch lay on the shelf, thin gold strap, small oval face. I picked it up and listened to it tick with calm precision. Time seemed to pass slightly slower and in a more orderly fashion for the owner of this watch than it did for me. Each of her seconds was measured and delivered to plan, forming an unbroken chain of identical seconds stretching in both directions without interruption or flaw. Perfect.

I could take this watch. The thought made my pulse skip and speed up. It'd be worth a bit. I could sell it. I glanced around the room, trying to think like a burglar. What else would I take?

My eyes rested again on the family photos. The man had his arm around the woman's shoulders and was leaning in towards her. She sat with her hands in her lap, not even trying. Not having to. The boy, he looked about six, was dangling around the man's neck like a monkey, grinning. One child. All the care and attention this couple had to offer lavished on this one lucky kid. Would they take something from him by giving him so much love and security? Perhaps he would grow with a sense of entitlement that robbed his own achievements of meaning. Or maybe it would all be peachy perfect. Could it ever be?

The peaceful atmosphere of the house was making me sleepy. I hadn't slept properly for weeks. The leather sofa looked too soft, too enveloping. The dining chairs had tall wooden backs and hessian covered bases and looked deliberately uncomfortable. I sat in an old armchair. And it was just right. Supportive, yielding, but not too much. Perhaps this was how a good man should be. Perhaps this was the way the man in the photographs was.

I could take the watch. I wasn't going to get anywhere with the referral business so perhaps I deserved to come out of today with something in my pocket. What would it be to the woman that lived here but a minor inconvenience?

But I couldn't. This fact annoyed me. I should've been able to. I should've been harder. What good were morals doing me exactly? Couldn't eat them. Couldn't burn them and warm my hands on the glow.

I put the watch back on the shelf and left the sitting room. I should've left the house altogether.

In the kitchen, glass bottles of different shapes and colours were arranged along the windowsill. The sun shone through them scattering patches of coloured light around the room, like pieces of a luminous jigsaw. Recipe books were bookended by herbs growing in terracotta pots.

There was a knife block in blonde wood, with protruding handles of brushed satiny metal. I drew one out. The metal was cool and silky against my palm. The bright sunlight, which danced with such sparkling enthusiasm over every reflective surface in the room, seemed to stop short of the knife. It pulled in close, drawn magnetically, but then hovered uncertainly a hair's breadth above the surface of the blade in a languid rippling movement, without making contact. The knife, although I held it firmly in my hand, was somehow unreachable, submerged in some other reality. I pressed the flat edge of the blade against the pad of my thumb. The skin bulged slightly. A slender white margin appeared between the metal and the raised whorls of my thumbprint. I pressed harder and the contrast between thumb, pressure-line and metal became more pronounced. Within the white border region, the spiralling ridges of identity became invisible. I pressed harder still. I don't know what I was hoping for but I felt sure there was some kind of answer to be had there.

When the pressure released, it did so with a sudden spray of blood that seemed to leap from my hand as though it had been straining to escape all along. There was so much of it so quickly, I could taste the dark, salty tang of it in the air. The knife clattered to the floor and the sudden noise focussed my attention back on where I was. In someone else's kitchen. Bleeding all over it.

I tucked my thumb into my fist but heavy beads still leaked through my fingers and splashed onto the worktop, the floor, down the fronts of the units. I grabbed a dishcloth and bound one end tightly around my thumb until I could feel my pulse beating within the cloth, then wrapped the rest around thumb and fist together.

It took me a moment to realise that the high-pitched wailing now filling the room was not coming from me.

'Come on, you. Let's get you cleaned up.' A female voice from the hall, raised above the gulping sobs of a child. The front door slammed. Perhaps it was only because I didn't move a single muscle, did not even blink, that they both passed by the kitchen without looking in. I recognised the woman from the photographs. I didn't get a good look at the child but the muddy, tear-streaked boy must have been her son. They carried on upstairs, the child's sobs subsiding into whimpers, the woman's voice a steady stream of reassurance.

The kitchen looked like the scene of some horrible crime. I left. I had to.

Derek and Joe were both sitting on the bonnet, smoking and talking. I heard Derek laugh his machine laugh. I stuffed my hand, dishcloth and all into my pocket.

'Here she is!' he called out as I approached. He rubbed his hands together and reached out for my clipboard.

Surprised to find that I did indeed have it, clasped in my free hand, I gave it over and watched him rifle through the unmarked referral forms.

'You're supposed to bring the signed copies back to me,' he said, frowning.

'I didn't get any.'

'What?' Derek exhaled noisily through his nose. 'Not a single one? Really?'

'Sorry. I don't think I'm much good at this,' I mumbled.

'Well, that's that then. Sorry, sweetheart, we don't do second chances. I'll give you a lift back into town.'

I stood there staring at him, dazed.

Derek gestured impatiently for me to get in the car. 'Come on. Take it or leave it.'

Back home, I drop my keys onto the table. The noise is immediately swallowed by the hungry silence. It prowls towards me – *is that all you've got?* For what feels like a long time, we circle each other, weighing up strengths and weaknesses, unsure who will win if it comes to a fight.

It's not what they take…

The dishcloth wrapped around my left hand is soaked all the way through and inside it's pulsing heavily as if I'm holding my own heart clenched in my fist.

The tension is finally shattered by the smallest of sounds.

A key in a lock.

10 Types of Mustard

The mustard is the worst part. Having to wear this Victorian chambermaid pinafore and not getting to sit down for hours – those things are fairly shit. But the mustard is the worst.

My heart always takes a dip when one of my tables orders steak. The mustard tray is silver-plated. So are the ten little pots and the ten little spoons. The whole lot must weigh about a stone and it has to be held one-handed because the other is needed to spoon out gobs of gunk next to the steaks. I can't put the tray down on the table because there isn't enough room and anyway, it's not allowed. I stand with the tray balanced on my arm, fingers curled upwards gripping the opposite edge to keep it all steady. It has to be held low, so the customers get a good view inside the pots. The longer they look, the heavier the tray feels. It's like their looking collects inside the pots, fills them up with something heavier than mustard.

Table five is taking the piss. I've been standing here for five minutes and my bicep is rigid and burning. The guy's steak leaks a thin pink fluid. His girlfriend's lipsticked mouth is losing the shape of a smile.

'And what's that one again?'

'Black mustard seeds you say? How intriguing.'

'Amanda, you simply must try the Bavarian!'

He knows what he's doing and he knows that I know. I see his type in here a lot. They're not here to enjoy the food for its own sake. They'd turn their noses up at the exact same dinner if just anyone could afford it. What they're savouring is the taste of their own money. But for some, that's not enough. They want a little side order of toying with the waitress to really bring out the flavour.

He's faking a connoisseur's interest. Enquiring into each mustard's finer points, licking his lips, smiling slyly at his companion as he asks me to talk him through it one more time. Amanda avoids his glance. He's trying to impress her but he's failing. One of the perks of this job, possibly the only one, is that I've become adept at reading body language. Amanda clearly thinks he's a dick. He doesn't realise this yet.

This secret knowledge gives me a glowing nugget of power. I swallow it down and, instantly, it spreads its warmth out and soothes the ache in my arm. Let him have his fun. That lipsticked mouth will not be going where he'd like it to go tonight. It'll be pecking him politely on the cheek at best.

Deep breath. Smile. From the top. There's – English, Dijon, Course French with black mustard seeds, Honey, Wholegrain, Arran with single malt, Irish wholegrain with Guinness, with Drambuie, Bavarian sweetened with applesauce, and Apricot with Ginger.

'Marvellous!' He leans forward nostrils twitching, waggles a finger over the tray and eventually settles on one. 'Wholegrain with honey?' he says, deliberately getting it wrong. Again.

The way Amanda sits back in her chair, repositions her napkin, still avoiding eye contact. She's distancing herself from him. She meets my eye for a fraction of a second then looks down to her lap again.

Sorry. I know he's a dick.

'That's the Irish Wholegrain, sir. With Guinness,' I explain. I give Amanda a raised eyebrow. *What are you doing with him then?*

She sighs and brushes invisible crumbs from the dark blue

silk of her skirt. *It's complicated.*

I flick a look towards the bottle of wine nestled in a bucket of ice on their table. It costs more than I'll earn in a week. I give her both eyebrows. *Yeah, I see that.*

'Splendid! Yes, I'll have a little smidge of that. And… Let me see…' He goes back to eeny meeny as I drop a yellow-brown speckled spot of the Irish next to his Sirloin.

Amanda huffily repositions her cutlery. *It's not like that.*

We both know she's not with him for his looks – thick-set and jowly, with a dirty blonde beginner's comb-over. It's not his personality, since his status as a dick has already been established. I glance at Amanda. *So?*

She examines her nail polish, gives an infinitesimal shrug and a wry twist of the lips. *Got pissed and slept with him by mistake.*

He dips his pinkie into the Irish and sucks it off, with fat little grunts of pleasure. Amanda's upper lip twitches. *Can't believe it myself.*

I let the little spoon drop back into its pot with a squelch.

Amanda closes her eyes and shudders faintly. *I'm not proud of it. But, he was so pathetically grateful. It would've been cruel to dump him straight away.*

'This one. Drambuie, did you say?'

I look at him, trying not to picture him all naked and needy. 'Well done, sir. Not many people have such a good memory.' I dole out a little splotch of the Honey mustard he's pointing at. He won't know the difference.

Amanda's gaze wanders around the room and settles on the wall clock. Her shoulders sink a little. *Only eight o'clock?* She twists her wrist to double check the time on her watch. An impatient sigh escapes. Her fingers tap a tiny drum roll on the tablecloth before she puts her hands in her lap and holds them there. *I'll wait until nine. Then I'll let him down gently.*

'Lovely!' He rubs his hands together and attempts a matey wink. 'I think that's all for now.'

I think so too. An inner warmth fills me to my fingertips and my arm feels good as new. 'Enjoy your meal,' I chirp, and head back to the kitchen.

White Pudding Supper

It's been mad in here today. I've not even had time to stop for anything to eat myself. I don't really mind though. Breathing in the smell of chips all day, it puts me right off. But see when you're hungry enough, there's something in that hot fat smell that gets right down your neck, just wraps itself round your guts and tugs. Same for anyone. If you leave it long enough, the hunger just takes over. But I missed lunch as well and I can get a bit nippy when I'm hungry, which is not the best idea for the evening shift ahead.

I break a stray wing of crispy batter from the edge of a fish and pop it in my mouth when Dino goes through the back for the sausages, then have to turn away and swallow quickly when he reappears. Eating behind the counter is absolutely Not On, and most especially not from any of the stuff on display.

We're stocking the hot cabinets, me and Dino. Mental hour is about to start. You'll have heard of happy hour in the pubs? Well this is nothing like that. Everything's the same price, just the customers are all mental cases. Not in the usual walking-around-like-a-normal-person-with-a-job-and-a-family-while-being-secretly-mental kind of way, but really properly mad, enough to have to stay in the hospital. What most folk, least of all the mental cases themselves don't appreciate is, they're the lucky ones. Mostly they're in there because someone is bothered enough about them to see they get locked up safely, instead of just leaving them lying in a pool of blood and sick in some doorway. If you've nowhere to go and no one to care, you've got to be a murderer or worse before you'll get a safe bed for the night.

The cases we get down here are bad enough to be in hospital but not scary enough to have to keep the doors locked *all* the time. So every Thursday at 6pm, they're allowed out to trail down the road in ones and twos and come in here to us. Sometimes I feel like a social worker or something, probably do more good than most of those arseholes, all those Fionas with their scarves and their earrings, and their 'self-esteem' and 'opening up' bollocks. If I had real problems, which I don't okay, the last person I'd want to talk to is a social worker. The very last person. You'll not get your dinner off any of them either.

I'm starting to feel a bit spaced out with hunger as I line up the scotch eggs and pies and I'm thinking about how my head sometimes feels a bit like a scotch egg.

My mate Gordon comes in. He's not my boyfriend, nothing like that, but we sometimes go out drinking and dancing, there's no law against it. He wants to know if I'm coming out tonight after my shift. I'd like to. A few beers would go down just nice but I don't get paid till tomorrow and don't have any money. Gordon says he'll sub me but I say no. Even when you're mates, if you let a guy buy you stuff, it gives them ideas, like they're owed something back at the end of the night and things can get nasty if you don't want to pay up. So now I always take my own money, safer that way. Me and Gordon stand outside the shop and smoke a cigarette together but I have to get back to work straight away. Gordon goes off in a huff. He doesn't say anything but he's got his hands pushed hard down into his pockets and he glares at his feet as he walks. Doesn't matter though, he's not my boyfriend or anything. I lift the hatch in the counter and go back to the staff side, close it behind me and flick the snib along.

The mental cases are harmless enough, once you get used to

them. There's the guy that mutters all the time, just a string of swear words and filth, but his order will be in there too so you have to listen to all of it really carefully. Some of it'd make your hair stand on end, but there it'll be, hiding amongst all the fucks and bastards, a little 'sausage supper, just salt,' and even a 'please, ya dirty hoor.' Then there's the Snow White couple who look like brother and sister, both with pure white skin, rosy cheeks and lips so red it seems like they must be wearing lipstick. They tiptoe up to the counter holding hands, stroking and reassuring each other, whispering their order and never looking anyone in the eye. The drooling man took a bit of getting used to. He just stares into nowhere with his mouth hanging open, a long thread of gluey dribble hanging from his lower lip and going down all the way to the floor without breaking. He shuffles forwards, his feet hardly leaving the ground and blubs out his order like a zombie, like someone else who's not even there is working his mouth for him. When he hands over the money it lands in my hand in slimy wet coins and I have to try hard not to look grossed out and just drop the coins in a paper cup next to the till for rinsing out later.

Anyway, I'm used to all of them now, and they don't faze me, I just get on with it. Live and let live. These folk have got enough shite in their lives. Tonight though, after the regulars, there's one I haven't seen before and I can tell straight away he's something different. He has patchy burnt-looking ginger hair and a beard to match and there's old yellow bruises on his face, but it's his eyes that bother me. They're black and he doesn't blink, just stares straight at me from the moment he comes in the shop and when he gets close, I can see behind them, like looking through smoked glass. It's like every strong feeling you could ever imagine having, and some you've only ever heard about, are all drunk and partying hard in the front room of his head.

I can see them all right there, fucking and fighting, crying and laughing and one figure in the middle of it all stands with his arms spread out on either side and his head flung back, covered in white fire, burning, screaming and burning.

He asks for a white pudding supper, salt and sauce on it, hands me the money. I give him his dinner wrapped in two layers of newspaper along with two pound change.

'I gave you a twenty,' he says, his voice like a knife. Some of the party animals behind his eyes stop what they're doing and stare out at me, like they're interested to know if they'll have to jump in.

'No,' I check the notes at the top of the till, there's no twenties, just an old crumpled five, 'that was definitely a fiver you gave me.' His face starts to change colour, blood rising up from under the old bruises, his eyes straining out of his head and suddenly there's a loud bang that makes all the pies in the hot cabinet jump. He's kicked the counter, just lashed out with his foot without taking his eyes from mine. The bang's so loud I'm wondering if he's wearing steel toe-capped boots. Has to be or he'd have broken something, he kicked out that hard. Dino comes out from the back of the shop wiping his hands on his apron.

'What's going on here?' he asks, looking between me and the mental case for an explanation.

'This little bitch is trying to cheat me is what's going on here! I gave her a twenty and she's pocketed it or something and is trying to fob me off with two quid, saying I only gave her a fiver.'

Dino looks at me, raises his eyebrows. He knows me well enough, so doesn't believe the guy for a second but his expression tells me we have to be careful and find a way of calming the guy down, or at least getting him out of the shop. Opening the till, Dino makes a show of poking through the contents, even looking underneath the grubby fiver. 'No mate, sorry, you must be mistaken, there are no twenties in here. I emptied the till myself just five minutes ago and there are none in here now so you can't have given her one.'

The guys just explodes. 'Fuck you! Fuck you! Fuck you both!' Spit flies from his mouth and he kicks the counter again, both feet this time, one after another, BANG BANG BANG.

Then he's jumping up and trying to reach over the counter towards me. I'm not sure if he's trying to grab me or hit me and I'm not keen to find out so I move sideways behind the hot cabinets. He follows me round on the other side but he's no hope of getting at me there since the cabinets are as tall as he is. Still, he's jumping up and pulling himself up on them. I can see his face through the greasy glass, all stretched and mad looking, reflecting off the sides of the case like his head's actually inside it, wedged between the onion rings and the jumbo burgers, his eyes glowing red and black like little round coals.

He starts in with his feet again. One of the panels on the customer side has been loose for ages. Dino keeps sticking big wads of blu tack behind it to keep it in place until it gets fixed properly but it can't stand up to this kind of treatment, tips forward and lands on the tiled floor with a hard crack, exposing the back of the deep fat fryers. The mental case looks like he can't believe his luck and starts laying into the stainless steel tanks with his feet, each kick making a deep booming noise. The hot fat inside the fryers leaps and splashes up from the open side next to me.

The attack on his fryers is too much for Dino. He lifts the hatch and moves around the counter, taking the guy by the elbow and saying firmly, 'Okay, pal, time to go. Come on, out.' He steers him out of the shop before he knows what's happening and when he does figure out what's going on and swings back round to push through the door again, Dino slams it shut and turns the snib so he's locked out. This really pisses him off and he shouts at the door for a while then takes a step back and to the side, opens the newspaper wrapper on his white pudding supper and starts picking chips out and chucking them hard as he can at the plate glass window. They bounce off leaving little splodges of brown sauce steaming on the glass. Dino waves him away but this just makes him even more angry. He grabs the white pudding and starts battering it against the window, all the while shouting.

'Bitch bitch bitch stole my money my fucking money my fucking money bitch burn you'll burn you'll fucking burn in hell for this thieving fucking bitch.'

Dino looks at me. Neither of us knows whether to laugh or be scared or both. The pudding is holding up pretty well considering how hard it's been whacked off the glass but after a while bits of fatty oatmeal start flaking off and sticking to the window, looking like bits of brain and the whole pane is shaking in its frame. Dino frowns and says, 'Think I better phone the police.'

They must have been close by because it's only a couple of minutes before two of them show up in a meat wagon. By this time, the guy has gone through the whole pudding, greyish lumps of it are sliding down the window leaving greasy trails. He's screwed up and thrown the empty wrapper and looks like he's squaring up to stick the head on the window instead when one of the uniforms collars him from behind and marches him into the waiting van.

Dino lets his pal into the shop and gives him a few chips while he asks us what it was all about. He nods and he tells us this isn't the first time they've taken this guy in for pulling the same trick. 'He's from the mental hospital up the road,' he tells us, 'and we know the hospital only ever gives them a fiver at most. Any more and they'll do something stupid, like buy booze or take a bus to somewhere and have to be brought back. Last time we picked him up he was trying to get on the overnight coach to Newcastle by holding the driver at gun point, only it wasn't a gun he had, it was a potato. And not a very big one at that. Poor sod.'

The rest of the evening is pretty dull. Dino puts the counter back together and cleans the window and we shut up shop. As I head down the road it starts to rain and the wind blows it right in my face. I pull my collar up and try to squeeze my head down between my shoulders. I'm thinking about the mental case with the white pudding supper and how he's probably nice and dry and warm by now in the day room, someone making him a cup of tea and asking if he wants to talk about it.

I phone Gordon when I get in. 'You still going to the club tonight?'

'Yeah,' he says, still sounding a bit huffy, but I can tell he'll get over it quick enough. 'I thought you were skint.'

'Well, I am but I think I'll come out for a few anyway. See you in half an hour.'

Round the back of the fire station, the neon club sign blurs red into the rain as I walk under it, Disco Inferno in big letters and a chalk board by the door reading 'Happy Hour 9 to 10pm'. Just made it. A bouncer with a shaved head and no neck, more fat than muscle, asks me for the entrance money. I reach into my back pocket and pull out a crisp twenty and hand it to him. I'm going to burn alright.

Human Testing

As if the space of a decade is no more than an arm's span across rumpled sheets, Ari reaches for him. And he is helpless. In exactly the way he always was with her, and precisely the way he should no longer be.

He struggles to remain in the present, where his new wife's voice now seems to come from far away although she's standing right beside him, breathing the same air filled with the smell of unpainted plasterboard. 'Maybe we should go for something more definite, more positive, like a nice bright blue,' she says.

His hands flap hopelessly over the colour swatches spread out before him as Ari reaches again from the past and draws him back across the years. Neutrals. Naturals. Warm Earth Tones. He is appalled at his own weakness. At how easily Ari accomplishes this trick of prizing him from the present, leaving his body dumb and empty-headed while his thoughts fly back to the past. He whimpers as he realises he will always be this way with her, defenceless, and she'll always be able to reel him back to her side whenever she pleases. His weakness bothers him especially because he does not consider himself weak. He plays centre back in football, is a tough negotiator of business deals, a stalwart friend and, most recently, a loyal husband. But with Ari… With her… weak as a baby. His lip trembles and he fears he may cry actual tears.

'These are all too wishy-washy, too vague,' his wife says, her voice receding as the distance in time between them increases.

His memory is definite. He sees Ari standing in the half-light of their bedroom, her arms raised above her head as she peels off her t-shirt. She hadn't meant for him to see the grid of small coloured rectangles above her left breast, like the rows of medals adorning the pocket of an implausible pastel General.

'What the hell is that?'

'Don't be annoyed.'

'I'm not.'

'Look, it's only a tanning lotion test. Nothing dangerous. It's easy money.'

He hated that she did that. Selling herself as a human guinea pig at that creepy lab. Most of all he hated that with him studying full-time, they needed the money.

'You don't know that. The fact they're doing tests means they don't know it's safe. How can you be so definite?'

'Human testing is just the last hoop they've got to jump through before they can license stuff. They've already blinded a whole shedload of bunnies before they get to me, if that makes you feel any better.'

She flops onto the unmade bed and tugs him down to lie beside her. And he buckles, just like that, down onto rumpled sheets, breathes in the familiar scent of her skin, now overlaid with unseasonal coconut oil.

'You worry too much. All that happens is they stencil some gunk on me and point a sun lamp at it for a couple of hours while I lie there reading a book. Then they give me money. Anyway, I think it looks cool. You should salute me, Private.'

'You look like a paint swatch.'

Ari giggles. 'Let's name them. Come on. We'll take turns. I'll go first.'

She presses one fingertip precisely on a pale yellowish rectangle in the hollow below her collarbone.

'*Morning Light*. This is the first morning we woke up

together. Remember? That first night you stayed over and when we woke it was already past ten and we laughed because neither of us normally slept that late or that well. We said we'd have to start sleeping together all the time, purely for health reasons. Your turn.'

He chooses a darker rectangle from the row below and brushes it lightly, surprised to find her skin cool to the touch.

'*Toasted Almond.* This one is the colour of the cake I made for your birthday. You said it tasted of cat piss, in a nice way, as if there's a nice way for cake to taste like cat piss. But we ate it all anyway. Every last crumb. Now you.'

'*Champagne.* This is the colour of champagne stains on Egyptian cotton sheets. That bottle we liberated from your pal's wedding reception and drank in bed back at the hotel. It wasn't real champagne, but we pretended we were decadent aristos and poured it into each other's belly buttons. Woke up all sticky. You.'

He is moving along the spectrum of pinks and browns towards the redder hues, testing their temperature with a fingertip as he goes. They are getting warmer.

'*Peach Blush.* This is the colour of...' He can't do this. 'This is the colour... No, I'm not... I can't. Sorry.' He can't concentrate. He hears his wife calling from ten years into what is now his future, latches on to the sound of her voice and drags himself hand-over-hand back to her side, to their present in that small unpainted room.

'Well you have a think about it. I need to pee. Again!' His wife sighs and stretches her arms above her head, her pregnant belly pushing out in front and for a moment it looks as if she is standing behind it and is about to walk off, leaving it draped in cloth and hovering in mid-air like a levitating crystal ball. But when she leaves she takes it with her.

He looks again at the paint swatches. Small rectangles of

creams, browns, pinks and reds rise and fall before his eyes, to the rhythm of Ari's breathing. Neutrals. Naturals. Warm Earth Tones. And again, he comes unstuck.

Ari says, '*Alabaster*. This is the colour of your face when I told you the test was positive.'

'I'm sorry.'

Ari says, '*Sugar Egg Pink*. This is the colour of the crappy carnations you gave me after you didn't come home that night. You couldn't understand why I was so worried and upset. I told you how love is carrying the other person around inside you so you're always with them even when you're not. You didn't understand. You still don't.'

'I'm so sorry.'

'Yeah, you said.'

'This one,' Ari says, now all the way into the reds.

'Please don't. Ari. Please. No.'

'*Sangria*. This is the colour of what you called The Only Sensible Option. This is the blood. Such a lot of blood. And you weren't there. You made me go through that alone.'

He bites his lip and tries to remember the future. If he could will himself there, be fully present in that small room with the smell of bare plaster. If he was only strong enough.

Ari says, '*Chilli Pepper*. You know this one. This is the colour of the mark my hand left on your face when you said afterwards *It's for the best* and *It wasn't meant to be* and *You'll get over it in time*. This is the colour of never getting over it, of never forgetting.'

His hands shake and his vision blurs as he tries to focus on the paint swatches he knows are there. He's looking for something now, searching for a shade definite enough to pull him back to the present and anchor himself there.

Ari says, 'This one?' She places her finger on the last shade, which looks sore and shows signs of blistering. 'That one will never heal. Even when it looks like it's gone, if it's exposed to the right conditions it'll blister up again, and weep.'

He takes a ragged breath and lets the paint swatches fall from his hand and leans his head against the plaster wall of what will be the baby's room. His baby's room. Now. Here, in the future.

His wife picks them up, straightening with a grunt of effort. 'Let's forget these,' she says. 'Let's go for blue instead. A nice strong colour.'

He can't speak so nods and wraps his arms around her and they stand with the future round and full between them, her belly pressed into his. When the kick comes he feels it almost as if it came from inside his own body. And he is helpless. Helpless as his wife laughs and brushes the tears from his face.

Ladies' Day

A wet, gusty wind barges across the race track. The women, the *ladies*, are woefully exposed to the elements in thin dresses that flick and snap around goose-bumped fake tan, not a coat to be seen, clinging on to head gear, reinserting clips and pins, trying to hold it all together. Three of us from the baby group – me, Kaz and Ashley – shelter behind a bookies' booth.

'Remind me again why we're here,' says Ashley, leaning on my shoulder for balance as she picks a wad of muddy grass from the heel of her stiletto.

Kaz glares at her. 'We're here to have a day off. We're going to have fun, right?' She scowls at the two of us until we nod agreement. 'Anyway, the tickets cost a bomb so at least pretend like you are.'

Ashley examines the muddy streaks on her fingers. 'I need a drink,' she says.

I give her a baby-wipe from the packet in my bag.

I should've phoned Kaz and said I'd got a cold, or Sean's shifts had been changed at the last minute. Something. Anything.

Sean had come up behind me as I fiddled with my hair in the hall mirror. 'Mmhmm. Looking good,' he said, wrapped his arms around my waist and pressed in against my back. His hands travelled upwards as he nuzzled into my neck.

I steadied myself against the wall. I'm not used to heels so my balance wasn't great to start with. I peeled his fingers off and wriggled out of his grip.

'Thanks, that really helps.' I tried a laugh to soften the sarcasm in my voice but it came out bent. I don't know what's wrong with me. My reflection frowned at us both from the mirror.

'What?' The mirror-Sean raised his open palms behind me. 'Well, you look sexy,' he pretend huffed, stepping back.

'No I don't. I look like someone's mum.'

The dress was bought for a wedding last year and was supposed to be *floaty* to blur the edges of my post-baby figure, but it just hung on me like a worn-out flowery dishcloth.

Sean smiled. 'You *are* someone's mum, pet.'

'I know that.' There was that irritability again, showing through like a spot under too much concealer. 'I meant someone older. Someone... else.'

A moment of silence opened up and out of it poured this sadness, like the sky had just emptied straight down on me. The anger washed away but I was drenched, the stupid dress drooping and dripping. I jerked in a breath and blinked a couple of times. Sean squeezed my shoulder and for a second I thought maybe he understood but I didn't have time to find out because there was a cry from upstairs. We both froze and tilted our heads to listen. A couple more whimpers and then silence. We looked at each other and nodded.

I went back to jabbing at my hair clips. Had I done them right? We were all supposed to have hats for today and I did try but hats make me look fake. I even tried a few of those feathery things Kaz showed me. 'It's a *fascinator*,' she said. 'Like I'm not fascinating enough already,' and laughed that loud laugh she's got, daring anyone to contradict her. All the time, this phrase, *morbid fascination*, kept pushing into my head and the fascinators, the *morbid* fascinators, started to look like exactly what they were: bits of dead bird. So, I compromised with these tiny enamel flowers, three of them in different purples. Hopefully they're enough to show I made the effort.

We make our way to the line of bars and food stalls strung out behind the betting ring, backing on to the red brick pavilion. Two plastic cups of fizzy wine pretending to be champagne and a double vodka later, the weather isn't so bad.

'Another?' I wave my empty cup at the others. I'd be feeling quite relaxed if it wasn't for these heels.

'Nah. Those prices are ridiculous,' says Kaz. 'Ashley, phone your Barry and get him to pass something over the fence for us.'

When the rumour had first gone round about security guards at the gates searching handbags and confiscating any alcohol, the options were discussed at our Tuesday afternoon baby group.

'You know if you open up boxes of wine, they have plastic bags inside?' Kaz had said. 'I could get a couple of them, strap one to each leg, up high so they couldn't be seen. They're not going to actually frisk me, are they?'

The other mums looked sceptical but cracked up laughing when Kaz stood up and waded around the hall like a fat gunslinger.

Liz, an old hand on baby number three, came up with another scheme. 'Those blue bricks you freeze for coolbags? Empty them out, fill them with whatever and stick them in with the picnic. You'd get a fair bit in that way.'

In the end, we didn't put any of the plans into action. We did get our bags searched though, which was just rude.

The Barry plan is a good one. If we keep buying drinks in here, I'll run out of cash before I manage to place a bet. I wouldn't bother, but it's not, strictly speaking, my own money.

Sean lifted his jacket off the banister and pulled his wallet from the inside pocket. 'You got enough?'

'I took some out of my account,' I muttered, looking at my shoes.

He knew as well as I did, there's nothing left in there. I've not worked since Tom. That was the deal and it isn't like what I do at home, looking after Tom, cleaning, cooking, all that, isn't work. We both agreed. It's fine. It's only times like this, not that they happen often, when there's something just for me and it takes money. I can't ask. Cannot force the words out my mouth. I'd rather go without than have to ask. I know Sean would never grudge me a few quid for myself, and I shouldn't feel this way. But I still do.

'Take it,' he said. 'Put a few bets on for me.' He was trying to make it okay by turning it into something I could do for him, like a favour, or a job. He understood that much. 'I'll expect a share of your winnings when you get back.'

He pressed the money into my hand and I took it, said thanks and shoved it into my handbag. There was an awkward silence and I turned towards the stairs. 'I'll just—'

'You'd best not,' Sean said. 'Don't want to wake him.'

'I'll be careful,' I whispered, already half-way up.

Tom lay on his back, arms thrown up above his head, as if the afternoon nap had taken him by surprise. His sleep breath snuffled in and out in a steady rhythm. I leant over the cot and felt that familiar desperate lurch in my stomach. Despite the satisfaction of seeing him grow, I can't help wishing he'd never change, that I could protect him from time and everything it'll bring, even though I know it's impossible and I've already failed. I reached a hand out to brush his curls but stopped short. Leaving would be much harder if he woke.

I stepped slowly backwards towards the door, in the pattern

dictated by which floorboards creak and which don't. Almost there, my heel came down on the soft toy from hell. It started up, high-pitched and insistent:

It's a small world after all

Christ, bloody thing.

It's a small world after all

I hear that tune in my sleep. I snatched it up,

It's a small world after all

and fumbled with the off switch.

It's a small, small —

Finally!

Tom turned his head and raised one arm, like he was waving, but his eyes were still closed and he puffed out a sigh and settled back to sleep.

Me and Kaz stand near the paddock, waiting for Ashley to get back, watching the horses being led in circles, snorting and stamping, manes knotted in bumpy braids, tails wound up tight. Women drift in and out of the betting booths and bars, carrying drinks and fluttering betting slips. The rain has gone off and a weak sun is making the grass sparkle. The scene looks almost like it was supposed to.

'That one!' Kaz shouts. 'We should bet on that one.' She's pointing to a brown mare skipping nervously around the paddock. The horse's skin looks tight and thin, every sinew and vein visible, eyes rolling, nostrils flared. As she goes past I catch a sharp whiff of sweat and earth and hot grassy breath. She's making a horrendous sound, chewing at the metal bar between her teeth. Flecks of white froth collect at the soft corners of her mouth.

'Why that one?' I ask.

'It just had a shit. I heard they go faster if they have a shit first.' Kaz folds her arms and looks knowledgeable.

'Well, less weight I suppose.' She might have a point.

'Perhaps we should try to scare another one,' she says.

'What for?' I ask, looking at the other horses, bristling with trapped energy. 'Why would you want to do that?'

'So they, y'know, go…?'

Sometimes it's hard to tell when Kaz is joking. But for once we don't have to stop and explain, or apologise. We're both crying with laughter, holding onto each other's arms, when Ashley arrives carrying a rolled-up cardigan.

'Guess what Barry says to me?' she demands, but doesn't stop for an answer.

Me and Kaz straighten our faces.

'He says *Talk about special treatment. You get to have your own day. Blokes don't get anything like that. We don't get Gentleman's Day.* Can you believe that? Poor you, I says, all you get is every other day.'

'What did you get then?' Kaz interrupts, plucking at the edge of the cardigan to reveal the red top of a vodka bottle.

Ashley steps away, pulling the wool back over the bottle and giving it a pat, cradling it like a baby.

An hour later, Ashley sits cross-legged on the tartan rug, one strap hanging off her shoulder, talking about her Barry and how he's great with the twins but the house will be a bombsite when she gets back. When she starts talking in circles, Kaz takes over about her dad's cancer and how her brother's no help at all since their mum's gone and she has to drag the kids backwards and forwards to the hospital. She talks fast, eyes wide, lips wet with vodka and coke. I think she'd like to stop talking because now she's rounded the last turn and we can all see what's waiting on the finish line. She stops abruptly and stares off across the track then knocks back the rest of her drink before clambering to her feet and swaying off to find the Ladies. I start talking about Sean and Tom and how I'm thinking of going back to work, which surprises me. I hadn't realised I was seriously considering it. None of us are used to talking without constant interruption from children. Combined with the drink, it's like running too fast downhill.

The horses thunder past, throwing up crescent-shaped clods of turf high into the air, the jockeys hunched on their backs in bright colours like parasitic beetles. The ground shakes, like drums from underground working their way up.

Kaz arrives back, waving a race programme. 'Right! We need to pick which horse to bet on. I think we should go for Liberty Trail, but I like the sound of Blue Tomato too.'

I pour more drinks and Ashley blows her nose.

'So, twenty quid each way?' Kaz pauses but gets no answer. 'I've no idea what that means either so don't look at me like that.'

I watch the horses as they loop back round for another circuit. I think I can see that mare from the paddock. She's out in front and my heart starts beating faster as I watch her straining ahead, a hurtling mass of muscle and sweat. She's tearing through the air, ripping it apart. It's like she's trying to tear a hole in front of her and escape through it, to some other place where something else, something more is waiting, a place where maybe she can stop running. It's always that bit further ahead. The promise of that.

Like Arseholes

MEGAN

The receptionist smiles and hands me a white address label with my name in capitals written across it in blue biro. 'If you could just wear this?'

No surname, although they've got my full name printed on the sign-in sheet. It's one of the ways they try to make everyone feel at ease. Doesn't work.

'If you could wait over there?' She nods towards a small group already installed in the far corner of the lobby, perched on sofas around a low table. 'Help yourself to coffee and biscuits. Someone will be down to collect you all soon.'

I join the three others, take my coat off and stick my label to my blouse. I scan the other labels. I'm rubbish with names but the faces look familiar, especially the old guy. Bristly salt-and-pepper hair, face red with broken blood vessels, silver-framed glasses digging into the soft fruit of his nose. Clean though. Polished black shoes and ironed jeans. Reformed alky? Name label says **ALLEN**. I've definitely seen him at one of these things before but can't quite place him. No biggy.

FRANCES

I remember Megan. Saw her few months back if I'm not mistaken. Had a thing about bananas. She's sitting quietly at the moment, but that won't last. She's right mouthy when she gets going, that one. Not that I blame her. It does make the time go faster when it's a lively group. Sometimes folk get all contentious just to keep themselves awake. I've been guilty of that myself, if not on the same scale.

Mixed genders this time. That can damp things right down, with the women just clamming up and letting the men talk. Depends. The older man looks like he'd hold forth given half a chance but that young one hasn't looked up from his phone since we've been sitting here. Hunched over, his big thumb stroking the thing up and down, only stopping to scratch his chin every now and then. Is that supposed to be some kind of trendy facial hair or is he just plain lazy, I wonder?

JAMIE

Shit. One bar? Fucking kidding me. Crap battery life. Defo changing my contract soon as I can. Can't get out of this one easy though. Fucking lock you in, eh? Thing is, there's always a better deal to be had somewhere else.

MEGAN

When you've been doing these things a few years, you start to recognise faces, although no one ever knows who anyone is, really. Everyone bends the truth to fit whatever the researchers are looking for. We all do it. My age has been known to vary by five to ten years either way. I've been a homeowner and a renter, had children and stayed child-free, been married, single, co-habiting, separated, divorced, had at least a dozen different jobs, and sometimes none. I've owned and not owned cars, smart-phones, compost bins, timeshares, stocks and shares. Name a popular product or service and there's a good chance I've taken a particular stance towards it. I have loved it, hated it and been completely indifferent towards it.

Don't think I've seen the young guy before. Maybe the middle-aged woman with the hair and the inch-thick orange slap on her face. Nobody is talking yet. We're still in the small smiles and nods zone.

I reach for a custard cream just as the woman opposite does the same.

FRANCES

To be honest, I've come to expect better. 'Bit sparse, this,' I say, gesturing towards the single plate of not-chocolate biscuits. 'I like when they have sandwiches and sausage rolls and those mini pork pies, that sort of thing. Saves me cooking dinner.' I bite into my custard cream. 'Doesn't do to pass up free food.' I smile at Megan. There's a girl who clearly doesn't pass up much in the way of edibles, free or otherwise.

She nods, her eyes widen. 'Pakora!' she says, spraying crumbs down her front. 'I was at this one once, had all this Indian food. Bajis and samosas and all that. Brilliant. I was stuffed.'

A shame the way young women let themselves go these days. She could be quite pretty as well. Lovely eyes. But the way her stomach pushes out over her waistband like that? Oh dear.

I look around at the group. Jamie is wearing a suit so has obviously come straight from a job, and not a manual one. I like a well turned out professional man, but his suit is in need of dry cleaning, his shirt off-white.

There's an unspoken agreement amongst the regulars that we don't talk about our real lives. So there's no real point in the normal kind of exchanges about families and jobs. The lack of proper information leads to speculation. At least it does for me.

The chat as we wait to be rounded up is usually about what other groups people have done, which was the easiest money, which had the best free food. And that's the way this is going. Megan's pakora outburst having broken the proverbial.

JAMIE

I put the phone on silent and join the chat. We can talk like this because we're out of ear-shot of the receptionist, not that she probably gives a fuck, and the organisers, whoever they are, haven't shown up yet. No idea what this one is for. We hardly ever know exactly what it is we're going to be having opinions about till we get started.

The one lie that you have to stick to in these groups, as far as the researchers are concerned, is the one about not having done anything similar before, or at least not for six months or a year. I had three groups last month and played the new boy in each one. We all do it.

'Best one I've had was the beer,' I say. 'Just sat on our arses drinking beer and saying whether we liked it or not. I mean, Christ, I'd do that for free. Easiest forty quid I've ever made. Thank you very much!'

ALLEN

While he talks, the youngster mimes drinking a pint, accepting money, tucking it into an inside pocket which he then pats in a satisfied way. Does he think we're all idiots or does he have some kind of miming disorder? Funny how you can go right off people, just like that.

Young folk these days have no conversational skills, they're only interested in performing. And even then, they're not interested in anyone's honest opinions. They just want to know that they're showing themselves in a way that others feel obliged to admire. There's no truth in anyone anymore. Nobody asks questions or cares to hear the answers.

MEGAN

Bloody typical. The guys always get the ones about drink. Like women aren't supposed to enjoy beer and whisky. Ha! Like the best we can hope for is that maybe someday Babycham or Lambrini might want to do a focus group on how to relaunch their fizzy pish. Gets my goat. The all-female groups are always about bloody supermarket shopping. Which bakery items would appeal to the housewife doing the weekly family shop? What kind of 3 for 1 deals would really get us splashing the housekeeping money? Have to bite my tongue in those ones, so hard sometimes it bleeds. Especially when I'm supposed to be a stay-at-home mother of three. What sort of fresh fruit do we expect to see available at smaller stores?

I remember Frances now. Her and her bloody bananas. Like they were the stuff of life. Got really heated about it. That and the ham. I mean, I just go to the shop and get whatever, not that interested. Some of these sad cows are actually driving between different supermarkets to get the best price on beans, or going out their way to go to a different one cos their husbands only like a steak pie out of that particular shop. Fucksake. Get a fucking life.

FRANCES

'Money for old rope really, isn't it?' I say. 'Just having opinions about stuff.'

Folk nod and smile but no one says anything. It's silent but for the sound of Megan chewing on what must be her third custard cream.

ALLEN

'Why are opinions like arseholes?'

It's a good question because it gives people a wee shake out of boredom, makes them pay attention and also makes them think. Not enough thinking these days.

MEGAN

Oh God. It's the arsehole guy. Now I remember him. This is his routine. He'll probably try and deliver the answer in his John Wayne voice.

I don't reckon Allen particularly needs the money. The intense way he talks, it's like these groups are his only real chance to be listened to, for his opinions to matter to someone. I bet in his real life he's one of those lonely old blokes who loiter at bars, forcing their conversation on anyone who stands still long enough. Probably, given that nose, over the course of his fifty-sixty years, he's pissed off everyone he's ever known. Could be he's got a family that doesn't want to know anymore and folk he used to call friends that are either already dead or are careful to avoid him in some other way.

ALLEN

'Everybody's got one,' I say, giving them my best Clint, 'and everyone thinks everyone else's stinks.'

All I get back are some half-hearted hahas from around the table. Honestly, you have to shove a rocket under folk these days to get a reaction. Although it does look like I've got to Frances.

I ignore her and carry on. Maybe I'll get some decent chat going. I lean forward. 'Everyone starts life as an arsehole. Did you know that?' They all look at me blankly. None of them has a clue. 'When a fertilized egg first starts to divide and cells multiply, they form a group, then a chain, then that chain curls round on itself into a circle but doesn't quite meet at the ends. It leaves a gap.' I demonstrate the circle and the gap with my index fingers, coming close but not meeting. People can always grasp a visual better than words. 'That gap will eventually become the anus.'

JAMIE

At anus, the fake red-head splutters coffee and clatters her cup and saucer down on the table. She's gone bright red in the face and she's coughing that hard her eyes are watering. Bit of an over-reaction. After all, he's right enough, we have all got one, even her.

The old guy pushes his glasses back up his nose, the pads sliding back into the dents on either side. 'First things first eh?' he says, ignoring Frances' wee choking fit. 'And the first thing is making sure there's an exit. A way out. Growth produces waste as a by-product and there has to be a way out for it or else the environment becomes toxic.'

I lean back in my seat. Toxic environment? No kidding. The old guy's breath is rank.

MEGAN

While we've all been preoccupied, wishing the arsehole guy would shut up or drop dead, a new member has arrived to join our group, taking up the last seat. The overstuffed brown upholstery gives a little pfft as she sits down.

The first thing I notice about her is her mouth. It's like she's not got one at all. Some trick of the light makes it look as if the skin below her nose continues smoothly down and wraps around her jawbone without so much as a wrinkle in between. I blink hard and look again. The illusion clears. She does have a mouth, of sorts. No more than an inch and a half across. It looks unfinished, as if it was added as an afterthought then abandoned before it was properly done.

She keeps her eyes down and crosses her ankles. Obviously new to this game. She's not going to be much use. Wouldn't say boo to a goose.

The whole point of focus groups is to have opinions and

speak up. You have to take your turn. Can't just sit there and stare at your hands. That's not what they pay us for. And if it wasn't for the money, none of us would be here. Except maybe Allen.

JAMIE

Christ, how long are they going to keep us waiting here?

I look at the three women in turn.

Aye... Probably... Aye, why not?

I'd do them all.

None of them are particularly fit or anything but I wouldn't turn it down. If it was there on a plate, like. No Sir. The older ones would be grateful, especially the fat one. Maybe she's a dyke. They don't bother about the fat the same as straight birds. The one with the orangey hair has the look of a screamer. But it's the quiet one with the small mouth that'd be the filthiest. It's always the quiet ones. I pass the time while the old guy drones on about cells and arseholes, imagining the women in various positions with each other, and me, obviously. It soon gets complicated. Imagining group sex is a bit like chess, holding all the possible moves and counter-moves in your head while not letting the entire plan go off the boil.

ALLEN

I give up. This new lassie's a waste of space. I can tell that straight off. Reminds me of my daughter, Lisa. Never could get a reaction out of her either. She'd just sit there, letting everything happen around her. Like her mother. Not one thing happened to that woman that she had the gumption to do anything about, not life, not death.

MEGAN

Either she's not been given a name label or she's not got the nerve to put it on.

There's one custard cream left and I'm just about to go for it when that bitch Frances picks up the plate, and offers it to the nameless girl saying, 'Here you are dear, you nearly missed the best bit.'

FRANCES

Anyone can see the poor thing needs that biscuit more than the rest of us. She's that thin, she'd snap in a high wind. The way young lassies starve themselves. It's not attractive. She could be quite pretty too. Lovely bone structure, if there was more than just skin stretched over it.

JAMIE

The skinny bird takes the biscuit without saying anything and starts nibbling away at it, like a mouse. Her mouth. Telling you. It's mental.

When it opens, you can just see, it's bright red inside. Can't take my eyes off it. Sexy as anything. All red, and wet. A tiny triangle of tongue darts out and swipes around her lips. I want to put my fingers in her mouth and feel about. Like there's bound to be treasure in there. Some kind of jewel or a golden key or a miniature beating heart. All this just comes out of nowhere. My mouth goes dry and I sit on my hands to stop them reaching out to her. I'm blushing. I glance around the rest of the group. Allen's glasses have come loose again and Megan is staring like she wants to eat her. Frances wipes her forehead with a tissue and it comes away all smeared with orangey-brown gunk.

MEGAN

We're all watching as she chews and swallows. It's like we're all waiting for something to happen. Then it does. She sits suddenly forward in her chair, her mouth peels open. I think she's about to speak. But her hand goes to her throat and her eyes widen. We're all just sitting there watching her. I'm hoping she's just making a big performance out of being about to speak, since she's said nothing so far. I think we're all trying to hold onto that same hope while knowing we're looking at something else completely.

ALLEN

Her eyes are bulging now, like they're being inflated from the inside, pushing out from the bones of her head and her hands are clawing at her throat, leaving red scores on her white skin. Her mouth is open so wide she looks like a baby bird waiting to be fed. Waiting and waiting and nothing coming her way. Straining wider and wider till her mouth is bigger than the whole of her head.

JAMIE

Why isn't anybody doing anything? I don't fucking know what to do. Why doesn't anyone know what the fuck to do? She's up off the seat in a crouching position, keeling over to the side and then she's down on the floor, her legs scrabbling under her like she's trying to run away. Then there's this moment like a pulse, like some electric charge goes through everyone and we're all on our feet.

FRANCES

Allen pulls the lassie upright and I get behind her, lock my arms around her middle and pull back hard. Heimlich manoeuvre.

Everyone knows it. Anyone of us could have done it. I just happen to be the one in the right place at the time.

JAMIE

This wet doughy wad of chewed custard cream comes shooting out the girl's mouth, hits the coffee table and explodes, sprays right across it. And it's like everyone unfreezes. Megan helps Frances and the pair of them lay the lassie down on the settee next to me as I sit down and let her sort of slump over so her head is on my lap. She's breathing heavy and her forehead is damp as I stroke her hair out of her eyes. She nestles into my arms like they're a space that was always waiting for her. I feel like I'll never let her go. Like I'm only here, was only ever here to take care of her. Like this is love.

ALLEN

It all happened so fast but everyone's doing what they need to do. I take the lassie's hand and rub it. It's limp but I can see the life pumping through those small blue veins. She turns her head and looks me right in the eye. Her eyes are so blue and her look makes a clear space right through all the shite and shows me what I have to do. Soon as I leave here I'm going to phone Lisa. Life is so fucking short. There's no time to arse around.

Megan has her arm around Frances, holding her up. Both crying. Big black tears are running down Frances' face and Megan is wiping them away, telling her everything's okay, that she's amazing, that she saved that lassie. Someone, maybe it was me, I don't know, shouts to the receptionist to phone an ambulance.

Chicken

Don't think about it. Just keep shovelling. Try not to breathe any more than necessary. Get the job done.

The stuff weighs almost nothing, taken one shovelful at a time. But when the first bag is full it stands as tall as my waist and the rolled plastic edges stretch tight over my fingers when I heft it to the side. One down, two more to go.

Across the road, I can see them watching. Arthur's orange curls blazing in the sun, legs planted wide, arms folded across his chest. He'll see these bags filled and brought back over the road and he won't take his eyes off me till it's done. No chance of escape. Not from him.

It's piled in three hills, high as houses in the middle of the field. This field isn't even ours. It belongs to the farmer next door but Arthur says we've an arrangement with him and I've drawn the short straw. What straw? I asked, and he gave me one of his looks. The short one, boy, he said. None of the others are going to stick up for me. They're having a great old laugh, happy not to be Arthur's victim for the day, the week, however long he likes. Eddie's been getting it in the neck most of the summer, so a day off for him must feel like Christmas. Still, someone needs to have a word.

Doesn't even smell like shit. Not like manure or anything. Manure's got a good clean smell, sort of natural. If I had to choose a favourite shit smell then it'd be horse. But this stuff is rank. Worse even than Eddie-after-a-curry-in-the-portabog stink. This is beyond shit. It's disease and filth. Don't get me wrong, I'm no veggie, I like my meat, but this stuff is making me think about the battery barns it's come from, about the crippled birds sitting in their own mess, about how all eighteen years of my life somehow add up to this. To me in this field with this mountain of shit.

Shake another bag open and weigh it down with a couple of shovelfuls. Where I've been digging, the stuff underneath is damp, yellow-white and porridgey. The sun has dried out the top layer and the wind lifts dust and crumpled feathers off the sides of the hills and swirls them around. It's all over me, on my face, in the creases of my clothes, through my hair, making it feel coarse and sticky like wool does when it's still on a sheep.

I blow my nose into my hand and this muck comes out thick like wallpaper paste. I hawk and spit and the taste in my mouth nearly makes me chuck but I hold it in. I'll not give him the satisfaction. Christ, it's hot. The sun's on the back of my neck like a branding iron.

Just get it done.

You'd think a man with a name like Arthur would be some nice easy-going old bloke with trousers all bagged out at the knee and maybe a fishing rod or an allotment. Our Arthur picks me up for work at five thirty every morning at the bottom of my street. The early start is fine when you get used to it. Better to be out the house before the old man wakes anyway. I like walking down the road while everyone else is asleep. Not a sound apart from the birds until Arthur turns up. I can hear him coming a mile off. Drives a red Escort with so many spoilers and extra bits of body-work you have to wonder what's underneath it all. When he pulls up, the engine noise is drowned out by the Bruce Springsteen Arthur likes to play, full blast with the windows down. He doesn't lower the volume when I get in, just shouts over the top of it, drinking from a can of Pepsi Max and steering with two fingers, arm crooked out the window. And he never stops talking. It's usually details I don't want to hear about all the sex stuff he did with his wife the night before. Or his psycho mates and the fights they get into. I just stare out the window, but I can't tune right out in case he asks a question and susses I've not been listening.

His eyes are a chlorinated blue, and his hair is brutally orange. No one takes the piss the way they normally would with a ginger nut. No jokes about Duracell or carrot tops around Arthur. Not if you value your life. Eddie once called him the Ginga Ninja, thinking Arthur was up the top field but he was back and he overheard him. Probably that's why Arthur's had it in for him all summer. Someone should say something though. He's right out of order.

Don't know what I did to deserve his attention today. Maybe he's just sharing out the pain, his own idea of fairness, showing he's no favourites.

His skin is white as milk, as if his hair and eyes got all the colour going and his skin was left with none. The muscles on his arms and shoulders are all scooped and piled up like ice cream Sundaes. He's not a tall man but not short. Broad, walks bow-legged like a cowboy, holding his arms out from his sides like he's about to reach for his gun any second. The rumour is he's not long out the jail. Killed some guy outside a pub. Didn't mean to, just unlucky. Not as unlucky as the poor bastard he killed, Eddie said. One punch and the guy went down, hit his head on the kerb and that was him. Finished. Involuntary manslaughter. I don't know if it's true. Don't know where the rumour came from. Could've been Arthur himself started it. It's the sort of thing he'd think was funny.

Couple of weeks ago he nailed Eddie's lunch box to the ceiling of the howf. We all watched him do it. No one said anything. He emptied it first, got the nail gun, stood on a chair, held the box against the ceiling and fired four nails through the base. Then he crammed Eddie's lunch back inside and put the lid on. When Eddie came in we all watched him looking for his lunch. Arthur watching us. Eventually he found it. Everyone was laughing, especially Eddie, though we all knew he didn't think it was funny. He saw it through, climbed up and tugged at the box so the lid came off, let his sandwiches slap him in the face, his banana poke him in the eye as it fell. He just stood there laughing, a brown smear of pickle wiped across his cheek. Never said a thing.

The empty box is still there on the ceiling. Eddie brings his lunch in a plastic bag now. And Eddie's the foreman. Arthur is really no one, no better than any of us, but don't try telling him that. Even Ross the Boss gives him a wide berth, calls Eddie up to the office if he's something to say, doesn't come down to the nursery himself if Arthur's around. Learned his lesson the first time. He'd said something about could Arthur please not park his car in his special manager's space. We all knew that was a mistake. Next day, Arthur got the guy that delivers the compost to dump the load on Ross's Beamer. Covered it completely, just the wing mirrors sticking out from this hill of compost. Ross got Eddie to dig it out. Didn't say anything to Arthur. Thing is, Arthur's a good worker, fast and strong, so we all have to work harder to keep up. Since he started we've got on faster than ever before. The top field is already laid out and the polytunnels are nearly done. That's pure profit for Ross. And that's what he likes. So, we're stuck with Arthur till the end of the season. All the same, it's not right. The way he is.

I'm on the third bag and it's started to rain. Not enough to wash the stuff off me. Just enough to plaster it on worse. The front of my coat is all stuck with scraggy feathers and crap, the combination of the wet and the dust making a kind of gluey soup. This lot is going straight in the machine, soon as I'm in the door. Boil wash. Just have to hope the old man's still down the pub when I get back.

It's not right though. I know fine nobody asked for three bags of chicken shit. Probably the farmer doesn't even know I'm in his field. For all I know he could come along and shoot me for nicking his shit. I shouldn't have to take this. But the third bag is almost full. I'll finish it. I'll fill these fucking bags and take them over and dump them and that'll be an end to it. And I'll tell him as much.

I have to take them one at a time. The wet plastic is hard to get a grip on and I have to hug them close in to my body, stuff falling out over my chest, some down the neck of my t-shirt. A car horn sounds as I cross the road, not looking, too busy thinking about what I'm going to say. I am going to say something. What's he going to do? I don't reckon he wants to go back to the jail. Arthur's watching me from a distance, smiling and nodding. His white t-shirt is tight across his chest, tucked into his faded blue jeans. He looks deliberately clean, glowing like a washing powder advert. I'm on my way back for the third bag when it occurs to me that maybe the jail is exactly what he wants. Maybe he's too much of a coward to face up to life on the outside. Maybe his wife and all the dirty stuff he claims she wants him to do makes him sick and he wants to get back to his quiet life inside. Provoking one of us enough to set him off. That'll be his plan. Mad ginger bastard. Well I'll not give him the satisfaction. No way. He can go whistle for it.

I've got all three over the road now and there's Arthur

standing with his hands on his hips, grinning like a pit bull. His eyes rake up and down over me. He licks his lips and winks. You've done a rare job there, he says. Good work. But there's been a change of plan. Farmer's changed his mind and we've to put it all back again. Guess who drew the short straw?

Eddie's in the background with the other two and they're all sniggering, scared to look me in the eye but watching all the same. Watching to see if I'll snap, if I'll say something. But I just pick one of the bags up, turn and start back, saying nothing, getting the job done.

The rest of the day is quiet. The smell coming off my clothes is disgusting. All I can think about is getting home and getting clean. So when knocking-off time comes and Arthur gives me a look and says, You're not getting in my car in that state, I'm about ready to lose it. But I don't. Fine, I say, no bother, and I start walking. There's no way I'll get home before the old man now.

Five minutes up the road and I can hear him coming up behind me, Born to Run fighting with the noise of his engine revving. It's winding up and up like one of those Hot Wheels cars you drag backwards on the carpet two-three times before letting it blast off into a wall or a chair leg. I don't even turn round, just keep walking. The rain has come on serious now. I stick my chin out and let it run down my face. He crawls up next to me, the engine noise dropping to a growl, and shouts for me to get in. I look round and see he's split open some plastic bags and laid them over the passenger seat. Come on, he says, don't be a dick, it's pissing down. A trickle of rain runs from my hair down the neck of my jacket. It's about four miles home, no buses. I think about it, think about how badly I want to be clean and try to weigh that against how much I don't want to be doing anything else today just because Arthur tells me to. He revs his engine again, flings the passenger door open, nails me with a look then pins it to the plastic-covered seat. I get in, say nothing. He drives, slapping his hand against the steering wheel, turns to look at me when we stop at the lights and shakes his head. Jesus, he says, the state of you. Then he turns Bruce up so loud there's no room for anyone else.

When we get to the bottom of my street he doesn't stop, just keeps going right past. You can't go home like that, he says. But he doesn't give a reason. And I realise, him not saying means he must know. He's heard it from one of the others, that the old man gets a bit handy sometimes. Right enough, walking in looking like a massive chicken's arse would be bound to set him off.

He keeps driving till we get to his house. It looks newer and neater than home, the front garden mono-blocked over to make a driveway for his car. Inside, it's all swirly carpets and velour furniture and there's no one else there. Thank fuck, no sign of that wife of his. I couldn't look her in the eye, the stuff Arthur's told me. Arthur seems different here, smaller, quieter. He shows me the shower, puts clean clothes out for me and leaves me to it. I'm not worried he's planning one of his jokes cos here it's like he's a normal person, almost.

I can't get my gear off quick enough. The only bad part is pulling my top over my head, getting the stink of it right in my face again. When I get in the shower, the warm water meets me and I lean into it and stand there letting it drill on the top of my head and pour down my body. Then I scrub and scrub till my skin's raw and new, soap myself with some lavender-smelling stuff I find in the shower tray, nearly choke letting the hot water run up inside my nose. But it's worth it, getting every last speck of that stuff off me.

I'm drying myself down, dizzy with the relief, when Arthur comes in and starts stripping off. He does it like it's a normal thing to do, like he does it all the time, so I try to act normal too, try not to stare. His body is all white knuckles of muscle and his hair is as orange down there as it is on top of his head. I try not to notice his long white cock, the way it swings when he pulls his t-shirt over his head. I'm holding my towel in front of me, keeping my own problem hidden, trying to will it back down. Arthur slaps me on the back, standing there with his nipples pale and rough-looking, like wild strawberries.

That's right, he says, you feel better now don't you? Even his voice sounds different here. He's not the same man he is at work. I nod. It's all I can do. His handprint burns on my back. And then his face is right in close, and he grabs the back of my neck in one hand and pulls me forward, pushes his mouth onto mine, forcing it open, tongue pushing past my teeth, stubble rasping against my skin. Just as our tongues meet, he pulls away and grins, his lips wet. Then before I can even breathe he pulls my towel away and looks down at me, sees what I've been trying to hide. Christ, he says, the state of you. And he laughs. He laughs loud.

He turns away, gets into the shower and closes the door. I can see his outline through the fogged up glass. He's singing, gargling Baby we were boh-orn to ruuun, lashing the soapy water over his shoulders. I start to shake. The room's full of steam and my head feels like it's going to burst. I see myself opening the shower door, stepping in, pinning Arthur hard up against the tiles, him pretending to struggle but not too much, me grabbing a fistful of wet orange curls. That's what he wants. But I won't give him the satisfaction. Then I see myself spinning him round and punching him hard, so hard, right in the face. I see myself watching as he crumples down into the shower tray spraying blood and teeth, waiting for him to get up but he never does.

I don't do either of those things.

I put the clean clothes on. They're far too big for me but I don't care. I find my crusty trainers in the hall and I'm out the door and running. I'm going so fast it makes my eyes water. My breath tears in my throat and the chicken-shit taste is up in my mouth again, this time mixed with soapy lavender. I spit but it's no use. Even if I manage to get that taste out of my mouth, I'll never get it out of my head.

I'm heading fast towards home and I realise, for the first time, I'm hoping the old man is in, and that he's had a few. Just let him have a go at me today. Just let him.

Odd Sympathy

Two pendulums when mounted on the same beam will end up
swinging in exactly opposite directions, regardless of their respective
individual motion, demonstrating 'an odd kind of sympathy.'
Christiaan Huygens in a letter to the Royal Society, 27 February 1665

I've been waiting for Kate at our table at the back of Viviani's for half a lifetime. My glass is almost empty and the ice cubes in her customary spritzer have eroded to smooth pebbles. Two waxy white flowers lean away from each other in a vase on the table. I'm not sure if they're real or fake and am fighting the urge to touch when the waiter interrupts.

'Would you like another?' He nods at my glass and smiles, showing straight white teeth.

'No, thanks,' I say automatically. I shouldn't. I'll be half-cut by the time Kate gets here. But then, so what if I am? 'Yes, actually, yes. Thanks.' The waiter removes my empty glass and raises one eyebrow enough to indicate that ordering by the glass will be indulged, but isn't fooling anyone.

I've been meeting Kate here regularly for years since we left university and she is always late. By my watch she's half an hour late already. I don't trust the new clock on the wall. I don't even like to look at it.

Time in Viviani's used to be measured out by the heavy tick-tock of an antique wooden clock. Today, without warning, an imposter hangs on the wall. Not clockwork, no checks and balances nestle within its casing. A quartz crystal machine of glass and stainless steel, hands driven by a cold vibrating light, it clicks with sterile precision. The disc at the end of its pendulum moves, unnaturally weightless, from side to side, scything the seconds away to fall in a heap on the floor.

Everything else is as it's always been: white tablecloths, scarlet fanned napkins, framed black and white prints of Roman architecture on dusky wallpaper, round backed chairs, the happy hum of couples and families, smells of fresh bread, basil and garlic blowing in from the kitchen like good news from home. Several generations of a large family talk over each other while the two youngest children, perfectly matched girls of about five, whisper over their spaghetti, small dark heads close together. At a table for two, a couple touch hands. Everything is the same, apart from the clock. The clock and me.

'Hey, Ali. Sorry I'm late,' Kate lands heavily in the seat opposite. 'Not kept you waiting too long though,' she adds hopefully, 'your glass is still half full.' I raise my glass and toast her, smiling, playing along.

'It's okay,' I say. 'I think my watch is running fast, so I'm probably early.'

Her smile falters a little. After so many years of knowing someone, the investment in each others' lives accrues interest and becomes a debt not easily written off.

Kate takes small sips from her spritzer and asks the waiter for a jug of tap water and another glass. We nibble breadsticks and look at the menu. We talk about her job in marketing and my sporadic supply teaching, the weather, the traffic, anything that doesn't really matter.

It wasn't always like this. We've known each other forever. Born on the same day, in the same hospital, it turned out our families lived in the same street. Growing up together, we used to pretend we were twins. We'd wear the same clothes and have our mums do our hair the same way. When one of us lost a tooth, the other would wobble and tug at their matching tooth until it came free as well, whether it was ready or not. Or maybe that was just me. I remember the dizzy elation of success as a miniature white trophy tore out, pinched between my fingers, the hot, metallic taste of blood filling my mouth, the tender hole in my gum that I couldn't keep my tongue out of for days afterwards.

No one could accuse us of being twins now. Kate is glossy, her long chestnut hair, swinging in thick waves down her back, matches her dark eyes and her skin glows. I lack the shine, the lustre. She is an abundant autumn harvest to my bleak mid-winter. I am brittle and dry as an old twig.

The waiter takes our orders and Kate absently rubs her stomach as he moves off. She's definitely put weight on over these last few months, while I have gone from slim, to thin, to bony. She notices me looking and colours uncharacteristically, looks away, then back.

'How are you doing, Ali? I mean, really? Are you coping? You don't look at all well.'

'I'm just tired.' This is not a lie. I don't sleep well and sometimes doubt I ever will again. 'Actually, I'm doing great. Really. Fine. I'm just getting on with things. What else is there to do?' This is a good and kind lie but does not satisfy Kate. There is more to come, I'm sure of it and equally sure I don't want to hear it. Our food arrives and, taking advantage of the interruption, I move the conversation on to her husband and that keeps her distracted for a while.

The girls from the family at the long table are giggling and posing for a plump aunt armed with a camera. 'That's it, girls. Oh, aren't you two just adorable?' The girls grin perfect white rows of still-intact baby teeth. Neither of them blinks when the camera flash goes off.

Kate is still talking, waving her fork in the air, but I'm remembering one day when we were five or six, walking along our street, holding hands and keeping step with each other. Mrs Breck from up the road went by pushing an enormous pram. Everyone knew Mrs Breck had had two babies but mum said they were 'far too early and she lost them both within the week, the poor, poor woman.' When we saw her with the pram that day, we thought she'd found them again.

As we ran towards her, she smiled at us in a hungry way that made Kate squeeze my hand and pull back, but I wanted to see the babies so dragged her with me to peek inside the pram.

The two identical occupants were wearing matching frilly white bonnets, tucked up tight together, wild-eyed and panting, their little pink tongues hanging out over white needle teeth, their dark, furry faces twisting from side to side. 'Look, Katie!' I gasped.

Mrs Breck tucked a scrabbling paw back under the white blanket. 'Aren't you two just adorable?' she asked her dog-babies. Kate nearly hauled me off my feet as we ran away. We never played twins again after that.

Kate is touching my hand and looking at me, head tilted to the side. 'Ali,' she sighs, removes her hand from mine and dabs the corners of her mouth with a scarlet napkin. She drops it, crumpled, onto the white tablecloth and I watch as it uncurls itself there, red spreading over white, like blood on hospital sheets.

'Look, I've got something to tell you and I don't know how to say it. It's supposed to be good news but what with... what happened, it's not the easiest thing. I wasn't going to tell you at all, but you have to know sooner or later, so...'

'Kate. What is it?' I ask, although I'm pretty sure I already know.

'I'm pregnant.' She looks at me hopefully, waiting for the

excited shriek of congratulation. When I fail to deliver, she continues as if I haven't heard her. 'I'm going to have a—'

'I know what pregnant means, Kate.' I force out a little laugh, but she's still deflated.

'Can't you be happy for me? I know it's not the best time for you, but you know we've been trying for ages and, well, it just happened. At last!'

I take a deep breath and give her what she needs. I do owe her that. 'Of course I'm happy for you. It's great! Really. Wonderful! I'm thrilled for you. How far along are you?'

'Four months now. I think it must have happened when we were in Rome for that week, so that would have been...'

Of course, Kate has forgotten. Why on earth should she remember? She wasn't there. 'April. That would have been April.'

'Of course – April, yes, I... Oh! Ali, I'm so sorry, I didn't think, I'm... Oh, this is all so hard! Everything I say is wrong.'

'Don't be daft,' I tell her lightly. 'You're being hormonal. I'm fine. Don't worry about me. I'm really, really happy for you.' I say it with feeling and I mean it. If only she had stopped right there.

'I wish I could do something. It must be horrible. But...' She seems to be gathering herself. 'I know this might sound a bit harsh, but if it does, I'm only being cruel to be kind. You do have to pull yourself together at some point. You can try again. The doctors said there was no reason you couldn't. I mean, there's nothing wrong with you. You were just unlucky.'

I could almost forgive her, even that.

'I know how you feel,' she says.

I can't look at her. Can't bear to see her face. Don't want her to see mine. If I look at her right now, she might burst into flames. I concentrate on the tablecloth. The hum of conversation around us drops and all I can hear is the relentless click of the empty clock. I stare at my plate and the breadstick I'm holding breaks in half.

She doesn't know. No one knows.

You lived for precisely one hour. That your eyes were the deepest navy. You were, for those sixty minutes, every one of those three thousand and six hundred seconds, the most perfect child the universe had ever witnessed before your small life flickered and went out. Like your mother, you arrived too early, but unlike your mother, you couldn't wait around. The sensation of my own heart continuing to beat in my chest has sickened me ever since I felt yours stop.

Instead, I take a large gulp of wine and try to keep my voice steady. 'I know. Unlucky, that's all. I need to move on. I will. I am.' I smile and knock back the rest, catching the waiter's attention for another refill. He notches his eyebrow up to the next setting but brings me another without comment.

For the rest of the time, I spoon-feed Kate the expected leading questions about names, colour schemes and people carriers and she happily chews over her pending domestic dilemmas. Eventually, my supply of questions begins to run dry and arid patches of silence open up.

'Oh god, I'm late.' Kate looks at her watch. 'I really have to run. I've got an antenatal appointment in half an hour.' I wave her away with a smile and she leaves, her meal hardly touched.

I push my own pasta around the plate. The girls at the long table giggle and feed each other ice cream with raspberry sauce from long silver spoons. Above my head, the wall clock's pendulum continues to scythe the seconds away. Our flowers are drooping and as I watch, one curled petal falls to the table and rocks from side to side.

Mezzanine

From the top of the racking, if you tilt your head and let your eyes go slack, you can see right through the perforated steel of the mezzanine floor, down to Groceries below. Then further, if you stay with it, through that floor to White Goods on the ground level. Must be, what? Sixty foot, give or take.

It's a rush, especially when I'm leaning out and holding on by only one or two fingers (the best way). That jolt of vertigo when the total height snaps into focus, the feeling there's only a few twigs of bone and stringy loops of muscle keeping me anchored to the living world. It's fucking terrifying. Makes me dizzy and weak but I do it every time. Because I can. Because I can feel all that and not lose it, not shake or cry or scream. I am in control.

There's that.

Then there's the feeling that comes next. Like I'm balanced, almost weightless, right at the very top of an idea so simple and perfect that it'll clear away all the shit in my head and make everything line up and fit together. That tipping point where all the effort of getting up there is over and the reward will be total lasting peace. Exactly there. That peak of anticipation before I go tearing down the other side, hair streaming, wind in my face, headlong into another brick wall. Not the Answer after all. Just another dud. I smash into but not through it. And I have to start again.

Can't

hang around here forever though. Work to be done.

Aisle 12. Kitchenware. Check my folder. Vyleda mop heads

- 3; mop handles - 2; Hozzlehock pegs - 2 standard size plain, 1 multi-coloured, 2 jumbo pegs with the springs. Section 7. Shelf 10. I don't know who racks the stock in the warehouse when it arrives but it's as if they deliberately put the difficult to carry stuff right at the top. Mop handles being a good example. The heads I can safely drop from any height and they'll be fine but the handles are different. Bits can get broken off. I have to find a way of carrying them down without losing my grip.

I leave the folder and clamber sideways, hand over hand, gripping the metal struts, pushing my toes between cardboard boxes for a foothold. We're not supposed to do it like this. Health and Safety and all that crap. But there are only so many ladders and so many stands and never enough to go around. If you always try to do things by the rules then you'll never get anything done at all.

My guidance teacher at school used to say if I didn't improve my attendance record and study for my exams then I'd 'end up stacking shelves at the supermarket.' Like that was the very worst thing that could happen to a person. Mr Smiley was surprisingly stupid. I remember I used to think teachers had to be clever, but the longer I stayed in school the more I noticed that most of them didn't have a scooby, and some weren't even half-way bright. That was a real

let down.

As it turned out,

I don't stack shelves. (Fuck you very much, Mr Smiley.) I'm behind the scenes, supplying those that do. I'm what's called a Picker. I write down what's missing from the shelves in a special folder full of plastic-covered shelf plans, using a special pen so it can be wiped clean at the end of each shift, then I go to the warehouse and load everything needed into tall metal trolleys and send them down in the lift to the shop floor. The shelf-stackers take it from there. I wonder whether Smiley would consider what I do better or worse than shelf-stacking. I wonder why I wonder that, because I honestly couldn't give a fuck.

I work from seven in the evening till midnight. The twilight shift, they call it. Makes it sound romantic and maybe a bit mystical, like we're a bunch of elves or pixies, tippy-toeing around the store in the half-light, sprinkling fairy dust and working our magic to make sure everything's perfect for the humans by morning. Hope I'm not bursting your bubble here but it's really not like that. No magic. No pixies. Just shit work and minimum wage. Same old same old.

Mum used to say 'don't pick it, it'll only get worse.' The phrase pops into my head every single time I clock on, like it's programmed into the card puncher. Card in, ka-chunk, fucking annoying advice out. It's irritating the way her nonsense hangs around, wormed into unexpected places, wherever there's a gap. It's like she's haunting me before she's even

    properly

    dead.

I stop for a little light refreshment. Section 5. Shelf 8. Still there. In a dusty old box of cracked draining racks that someone should really throw out, a half bottle of Bell's, tucked down the side. The very thing. Onwards. I take a wide swing out, one arm gripping, the other swooping in an arc. As a species, we should've stayed in the trees. There's something about climbing like this. Feels somehow real.

Mum also used to say 'little pickers wear bigger knickers.' Never mind big knickers, I'm wearing cycle shorts under my blue polyester uniform skirt. All the female pickers learn that on their first shift. When you're high in the warehouse racking, even if you use the ladders like you're supposed to, there'll always be some smartarse down below ready to pass comment. Be easier if we could wear trousers, but that's against the rules too. Not a big fan of the rules, me.

Right on cue, I get a drawn-out, sarcastic wolf whistle from Davey, pushing a trolley below where I'm pulling packets of pegs out of a box. He hasn't stopped, or even looked up properly, it's just a reflex.

'Away and piss off!' I shout down. Doesn't cost anything to be polite.

'Love you too, Babe,' he calls back over his shoulder, still pushing his trolley towards the lifts.

'Jackie,' I call after him. 'My name is Jackie.'

Davey's alright. Some of the others aren't, which makes Davey a Good Guy. The clunk and rattle of his trolley wheels dwindle away to nothing, lost in a few turns of the high-sided cardboard maze.

I drop the three mop heads, one after another and they land with soft thuds. The wooden pegs can be safely dropped as well but not the plastic ones, they're likely to break. I start wrestling the mop handles out of their box. At least there's only two. Heads wear out quicker than handles. Shame people don't have replacement heads for when the ones we've started out with get knackered or worn out. Folk could have a collection of spare heads for different occasions. A head for every day of the week. Useful for those difficult mornings too. Which might not be quite so difficult if I stopped drinking so much. But the thing about drinking,

proper drinking,

till I'm almost-passing-out (but not), is that I get close to the edge,

which is the only place I can feel

alive.

No matter how smashed I get, no matter how physically incapable, there's always part of me sitting in a corner of my head, calmly watching, absolutely sober. Nothing can touch that part of me. Nothing. It's cold. Immune to everything (I've checked it all). I like to get close to it so I can remind myself it's still there. I'm still there. Standing near

the edge

is the only place I can get a grip, feel the shape of things, feel my hold on them.

I wedge the two mop handles under my arm and start climbing down, pausing at each shelf to move the packets of plastic pegs down as I go. It's tricky. My arms are getting tired and the mop handles keep catching on the racking and threatening to lever me off into thin air. But I've done this before. I can handle it.

It's always better to visit the edge deliberately than to wait for it to come and find me. Often, it arrives without warning. I wake up and it's right at the side of my bed and just putting my feet on the floor is taking a step off a cliff, off the edge of the world into endless black space, and I've no idea when or

if

my feet might land again on solid ground.

Made it. I stack everything together on my trolley and take a moment to roll my shoulders, stretch my arms out, imagine them growing and spreading out and out and up and up.

And sometimes the edge stalks me all day, lurking under kerbs waiting to snatch at my ankles when I cross the road, or in the lift shaft where the lift should be but hardly ever is, waiting to suck me down. Or in the silences I don't know how to fill when people talk to me. Wherever there's a

gap.
It could be

anywhere.

My mother came out through the gaps between her father's words and what his silences admitted. I met him, that once, though she didn't want me to. 'There's nothing to be gained,' she said. Another of her ready-made phrases. Her speech was always full of them. She hardly ever put words together herself. Her talk was all verbal chicken nuggets – bland, bite-sized and pre-processed. Now she's even lost the ability to choose the right one for the occasion. She'll sit there and smile vaguely, her eyes drowning in themselves, and say things like 'you'll catch your death' and 'what a wicked web we weave…' then trail off and start humming some never-ending tuneless tune.

Lately she doesn't seem to care who I might be but sometimes she hazards a few guesses. Some of the names she comes out with – I'm sure she's never even met folk with those names, she's just pulling them out of the air, or maybe from memories of TV soaps.

Mary? Trisha? Amelia? Gracie?

'Jackie,' I tell her. 'It's Jackie.'

She looks at me and frowns like she's searching through the clutter in her head and I think maybe she's going to find me in there somewhere, but she just shakes her head and says, 'A little knowledge is a dangerous thing.'

Finding him was easier than I'd imagined it could be. He wasn't even bothering to hide. As if he had nothing to be ashamed of.

I went to the pub first, steadied myself, then went and sat in his piss-smelling front room and watched as everything I didn't know but half-suspected about my mother's childhood came hissing like steam out through his words and formed the shape of a girl struggling to disappear. He gave me a battered box-file of papers, old photos and letters. Said he had no use for them anymore and I may as well take them away. Pandora doesn't know the half of it. Inside that box were packed the overlaid shadows of those who came before him, like a lesson in cause and effect. All the generations rising up out of it until they clenched together and swung

back down,

like a fist coming right at

me

on the mezzanine floor. I start climbing again. I feel better up high and I left the stock folder up there anyway.

There are holes in everything. Holes, in fact, if you want to take it all the way (and why wouldn't you?), are what the world and everything in it is made of. I've been thinking about this. Atoms, right? They're mostly empty. Electrons and whatever else, whizzing around a big load of nothing. So, the truth of it is, there's more nothing than anything else. There are more gaps than not-gaps, more holes than

Mum still likes to crochet. She's rotten at it but never lets that stop her. She makes squares with different patterns in endlessly ugly colour combinations then sews them together to make scarves and tea cosies and cot blankets. The results were always misshapen and full of holes but they've got a lot worse recently. Holes are what they're made of now, loosely strung together with wool.

There were similarities. Of course. You can't get away from genetics. It's inheritance. Passed down, hand to hand, one to the next. He was old, but still managing to live on his own. He looked at me as I was leaving, sniffed the whisky on my breath and said, 'the apple never falls far from the tree.'

And what a tree it is. Our family tree. Maybe every family is the same if you peel back the bark and inspect the wormholes. Maybe we all come from the same long line of broken minds, drunks and bastards.

It's like some kind of optical illusion, seeing all the stories layered on top of each other, snapping in and out of focus. Like there's a hidden meaning in the way the pattern shifts, some secret to be revealed from the way new patterns develop.

I climb

back to Section 5, shelf 8 and the bottle's near enough empty now. Might as well finish it off. The racking lurches to the side as I stash the empty bottle back in the box but I don't let it faze me. The effects of that joint I smoked in the car park are joining forces with the whisky now, setting the outer edges of my perception spinning like a wobbly carousel. I look down and watch the racking twisting round on itself, groaning under the strain into a spiralling ladder of metal. Not even going to try and get down that.

I go sideways again, find that narrow gap at the very top of Section 9 and crawl in, shoulders brushing against the boxes on either side. Just a short break and I'll get back to work. It's not bad here. Quite cosy. I could have a nap. No one would notice.

The sober part of me that's been observing, taking notes, agrees. Sleep would be a Good Thing. In my dreams,

I'm always
climbing.

Rubble

Matthew, who knows his name only as a sound his mother often makes, sits and looks at the thing in his hand. He doesn't have the words to describe its shape, colour or texture. To you or me, this would be a red wooden cube with sides about two inches long. And that's all it would be. Matthew, however, holds infinite possibility in the palm of his hand. He lifts it to his mouth, sucks a corner and discovers it is not a thing for eating.

Another cube nearby looks almost exactly the same, but this one is more like outside. We'd call it green. Matthew crawls over and grasps it in his free hand. This is not for eating either.

He drops one cube on the carpet and looks at the other in his hand, then back at the one on the floor and an idea begins to form. He feels it swelling in his mind, like an enormous bubble. This idea is so big, so shiny, he doesn't dare blink in case it bursts. This is important. Slowly, so slowly, he lowers one cube until it rests on top of the other and then he takes his hand away. Nothing will ever be the same again.

In the kitchen, Matthew's mother is unaware of her son's discovery. She's pacing back and forth with the phone jammed to the side of her head, her whole body tilted towards it, as if this will help make sense of what she's hearing.

'Not coming back? What do you mean, Not coming back?' she says. She tries to think behind his short sentence, to prise the words apart and find the alternate meaning that surely must be hidden somewhere.

There's a long silence. She puts the phone down and leans her forehead against the cupboard door, presses hard and rolls it from side to side, focusing on the small, controllable pain this produces. There's no time to think. It's past eight o'clock and they should be on their way.

She splashes cold water on her face, locates her work shoes, bag and keys and goes into the front room for Matthew. At any other time, she would've paid attention, would've knelt on the floor and been properly impressed. But not today. Today, she scoops him up before he succeeds in placing brick number three and a cube of blue, bright as a summer sky, falls from his hand and rolls across the carpet. Matthew twists and wriggles. He stretches out his arms, fingers straining, and howls in protest.

With Matthew securely strapped into the back seat, Melanie joins the rush hour traffic which turns the five-minute journey to her sister's house into twenty. The windows of the corner shop have been smashed again. Boards have been hastily hammered in place and stare out over the shattered glass still strewn across the pavement. The place already looks abandoned.

She concentrates on the day ahead. Another day of job hunting. She doesn't enjoy deceiving Karen, dropping Matthew with her and heading off as if she was going to the office as usual, but if she lets go of the routine, anything could happen.

The lights at the crossroads cycle back to red but the queue doesn't move forward. She sighs and opens the windows a crack. Off her passenger side, the wall surrounding the vacant lot has a hole in it about four feet wide into which a flimsy wire fence has been crammed. A sign hangs lopsided from the wire bearing a one-word message – Dangerous.

Beyond the fence, an expanse of rubble stretches out in mini-ranges, weeds sprouting between the low mounds. There's a movement at the edge of her vision and a dry, shifting sound as a small landslide spills pebbles down one of the slopes. Just the ground settling, a cat perhaps, or children playing where they shouldn't. That sign would be a magnet to some. The movement comes again, this time on the far side of the empty lot. Too big for a cat, or a child, a rolling wave that sends earth and stones tumbling from the peaks. She imagines the rubble as a living thing, a massive creature looking out at the traffic and shrugging its shoulders in puzzlement, or simple indifference.

Perhaps the fence and the sign aren't to stop people getting in, but to stop whatever's in there from getting out. Maybe the real danger is that the rubble may rise up and break out, inciting a revolution of collapse which would sweep through the streets in an orgy of destruction, calling other buildings to join it, pulling down garden walls, factories, empty offices, dilapidated warehouses into the boiling tide. Some structures would need very little encouragement. Others might seem stable enough but they too would succumb eventually. Ruin is innate and inevitable in all things. Everything disintegrates.

A car horn blares behind her. The lights are green.

She thinks about their last holiday. She'd been six months pregnant with Matthew and the idea was to spend some time together before the baby arrived. The island was a parched, dusty tourist trap of bars and dirty beaches, the air slimy with coconut suntan lotion and frying fat. Between the concrete blocks of hotels and the beachfront restaurants were stretches of wasteland that nobody claimed, full of rubbish and rubble and starving, thorny weeds. These patches of forgotten land disturbed her. If you stepped into one, you might not be seen again.

The heat was unbearable and she feared the baby would cook inside her. She tried to stay in the shade, switching seats in the cafés as the sun climbed overhead and the line of blinding heat advanced across the tables. Gazing out across the dull pewter

Atlantic to an indistinct shape on the horizon, she asked, 'Is that another island?' He shrugged and made a 'Phff' sound. She asked what he thought was beyond the island. 'The end of the world,' he answered, without hesitation. There was no question in his voice, no hint of an upward inflection to soften the blow. They sat and looked at it and she knew from that moment the end was coming. Still, his timing could hardly have been worse.

Karen's house is full of primary colours and children and smells of toast. Her two eldest are playing with Lego in the conservatory while Karen changes the baby's nappy.

'There! Doesn't that feel better? Yes. It. Does.' Karen punctuates her speech with play pinches of the boy's fat cheeks. He squeals with laughter as she picks him up and slings him over one hip. 'Jesus, Mel,' she says, giving her sister a searching look, 'you look like crap. You okay?'

Melanie rubs a hand across her forehead. 'I'm fine. Just tired, y'know?'

Karen puts the baby down in a bouncy chair and reaches for Matthew. 'Have you been keeping your mummy up at night, you little monster? Well, you know what we do with monsters here?' She blows a noisy raspberry on Matthew's neck and he squirms and giggles. 'When does that man of yours get back anyway? Or is he inventing more work just to dodge the night shift?'

Melanie sighs. 'Well...'

A fight suddenly erupts in the conservatory over who has the most sloped bits for the roofs. There are never enough of those bits, she knows. Nathan, four, an advocate of direct action, has smashed up the house his older sister Chloe was building. In retaliation she has pushed him over and he has landed badly on his garage and is now wailing, 'Mummeeee!'

Unflustered, Karen makes for the war zone. It lights her up, thinks Melanie. 'Organised chaos!' Karen exclaims, as if that were something to be enjoyed.

Melanie backs away. The concept makes her nauseous with dread. 'I better get going,' she says.

'It's not fair!' shouts Chloe. 'He always ruins everything!'

'Shush now,' says Karen, rubbing Nathan's legs as he snivels. 'Why don't you two build something together?'

'No no no!' they yell, at once in complete agreement.

Karen looks up at her as if surprised to see her still there, hovering in the doorway. 'Okay then. See you later. Don't work too hard.'

Melanie arrives at the office on time and parks by the security gate. There's no reason to keep coming back but every morning, when she tries to think of what else she might do, where else she might go, she finds only an empty space in her mind where the answer should be. She hadn't liked her job but now it's gone, as well as the pay check, she misses the familiar battles and tired jokes, the mud-coloured coffee, even her boss's bad breath. She has hardly any savings and unless she finds another income soon, things will start falling apart.

The roof of the office building has been removed since last week and the interior gutted. A new sign on the security gate reads Keep Out Demolition in Progress below a black exclamation mark in a yellow triangle.

After a few minutes, she drives away and heads towards the ring road. The traffic is heavy. People with jobs hurrying from one task to another, going to meetings, chasing deadlines, delivery times, opening hours. Or perhaps they're like her, driving for a sense of purpose, desperately trying to join the dots from A to B to give their day a shape.

She pulls out into the fast lane but red brake lights are going on in pairs as far as she can see. To the left, a sign reading Diversion crawls by, followed by another. Up ahead she sees an indistinct shape stretching across both lanes. It looks impossibly like a small hill or an island wreathed in sea-mist. As the traffic creeps closer, the shape solidifies into a pile of rubble and the mist turns to dust. She flicks on her wipers and they drag grit from side to side across the windscreen.

Before they reach the obstruction, traffic cones herd them off onto a slip road. She stares at the rubble as the line veers away from it. There's too much to be the result of a lorry shedding its load. Sweat prickles on the palms of her hands. In the car in front, a woman is talking on her mobile. Behind, a van driver taps his hands on his steering wheel in time to music she can't hear. They have their eyes on the road ahead. Just another diversion. No big deal.

She pulls into a transport café, orders coffee, buys a newspaper and searches for the Situations Vacant page but finds only endless cars for sale. She wonders how much she'd get for hers.

There's a dull thunk on the table as a small cube of plaster, about two inches square lands next to her coffee cup. She looks up. The ceiling of the café is veined with thick cracks extending the length of the room. As she stares, the cracks bulge and spread as if the emptiness they contain is liquid and pulsing, alive.

A waitress with sad eyes and pink lipstick stops beside her table and drags a dirty cloth across the Formica, scooping up the lump of plaster. Melanie opens her mouth to speak but the waitress has already moved on.

She is still gaping at the ceiling, wondering why no one else seems to have noticed what's going on, when the far side of the café collapses with a grinding crash. She jumps to her feet, spilling her coffee. Was there anyone sitting over there? Shouldn't somebody do something? She coughs and wipes her eyes. Through the cloud of dust she sees the waitress shake her head and fetch a mop from behind the counter. A man in overalls belches.

She staggers out of the groaning building, gasping for breath. There are no emergency vehicles, no one is running or screaming. She licks her lips and tastes stone. Cars glide by, the occupants oblivious. She stares at the flow of traffic and it becomes hypnotic, calming. Before long she decides she wants nothing more than to join it.

On the outer bypass, all is serene. Four lanes of smooth running order cut through the green belt, two in one direction and two back the other way. Perfect balance. She thinks only of her wheels pressed firmly to the road, holding a steady course. She doesn't think about how to keep Matthew in nappies and food when there's no money. Instead, she clears her mind, tunes her thoughts to the drone of rubber on tarmac.

She has been travelling this way for some time when the comforting hum is knocked out of tune. A deeper bass note is insinuating itself upwards, getting louder. A growling, tearing thunder eating away her equilibrium.

A dark shape appears on the horizon, moving towards her on the opposite carriageway. A truck? No, too big, and black all over. No windows. No driver. No wheels. It grows in size, dwarfing the cars in front of it before rolling right over the top of them, grinding them to dust.

Dear God. Doesn't anyone else see it?

She waves frantically to the drivers in the cars coming towards her, flashes her lights and points behind them. Some look at her curiously, most ignore her. She can feel the bone-shaking rumble through the wheels of her own car. The black shape is nearly level with her as it smashes a young couple in a red hatchback into oblivion. One second they were laughing together at some shared joke, him reaching his hand out to rest on her knee, the fall of her hair half-hiding her smile, and the next they were slapped out of existence.

The whole carriageway is rolling itself up like a monstrous Swiss roll, black tarry stones spraying from the wheeling edges as it passes. At least forty feet high, it casts an immense shadow. Her hands are shaking as she grips the wheel and it feels like something is tearing loose in her chest. Something necessary. Something she can't afford to lose.

In her rear-view mirror she sees the shape carrying on, crushing everything in its path. She looks at the face of the driver behind her. He is picking his nose and flicking the result out of his window. She looks further back, searching the horizon where the road meets the sky and it isn't long before another dark shape appears. This time on her carriageway.

She swerves towards the inside lane, narrowly missing another car. Ignoring the angry gesticulations of the other driver, she pulls off onto the hard shoulder, then further onto the grass. She clambers out and manages a few stumbling steps before falling to the ground, which is shuddering beneath her. The road she had been driving on only moments before, rumbles past like a giant wheel of liquorice, leaving in its wake an uneven surface of stones and gravel and a thick, tarry stench.

Nothing moves.

The ground that used to be road glitters with shards of broken glass and metal. Fragments of mirror sparkle in the sunlight and reflect tiny bits of broken sky.

Melanie turns away, pulls herself to her feet and staggers to the top of the verge. On the far side, the landscape falls away towards the city, its tower blocks and spires, its networks of houses and parks, its familiar comforts. Then she notices a cloud of dust hovering over the eastern edge of the city and where there should have been houses, there are only shifting areas of grey and brown, rising and falling like waves. A factory chimney collapses in on itself and joins the tide pushing westwards across the city.

Matthew!

Karen's house is to the south-west. Panic swallows her in a single gulp and she reels, reaching out for support that isn't there. Oh please God, let him be okay, let them all be okay. Karen, the kids. She'd give anything. *Anything*. She has to get to them before the tide crosses the city.

Her car is still on the verge, untouched by the passing carnage. There is no road to drive on but she rolls back down the grassy bank and onto the track where the road had been. She prays her tyres will last long enough as she drives on, skidding and fishtailing, her teeth clacking together as her body is flung around inside the car like a pea in a whistle, while her fingers grip tightly onto the steering wheel.

At last a slip road, and it still has tarmac. She takes it and enters the city, which is inexplicably going about its normal business. Mothers push buggies, workmen drill holes, shoppers shift bags from hand to hand, for all the world as if this was a normal day. Something in the dust, she decides. Some kind of psycho-active chemical that's keeping everyone sedated, unaware of what's going on. She rolls both her windows up and takes shallow breaths. She has to get across the city to her family. Let the rest of the world fend for itself.

She barrels down one way streets, runs red lights, leans on her horn and swerves around other cars. It seems to go on for hours. When she eventually arrives in Karen's street, she presses her forehead briefly to the steering wheel as if giving thanks to the car for delivering her safely this far.

She gets out of the car and everything seems so completely normal that she's almost willing to believe she imagined or hallucinated the whole thing. The street is entirely intact. But then she sees the dust cloud on the horizon, to the east.

She runs up the path and hammers on the door. 'Karen, come on!'

Her sister opens the door. 'Mel? What on earth?'

'Get the kids, we've got to get out of here. Fast. Where's Matthew?'

'Having lunch. What's going on? What's happened? Melanie! Talk to me! What's wrong?'

She pushes past Karen and runs through the house into the kitchen. The kids are at the table, Matthew strapped into a high chair, merrily decorating his face with food. She grabs him and tries to pull him out of the seat, forgetting to undo the straps. He squeals and starts to cry. 'It's okay baby, it's okay. Mummy's here. It's going to be okay,' she says, and fumbles with the buckle.

'Mel!' Karen's hand is on her arm. 'Stop it. You're scaring him.'

Karen's children are staring at Melanie, wide-eyed and pale, food forgotten on their plates. 'Now,' says Karen in her best no-fuss voice, 'let Matthew finish his lunch and you come with me and tell me what's going on.' She peels Melanie away from Matthew and says to the kids, 'Don't worry, Auntie Mel's not feeling well, but she'll be fine in a minute. Finish up your fish fingers now.' Karen leads her gently but firmly out of the kitchen.

She can't stay still but Karen forces her to sit down and explain. In a rush she tells her everything she's seen and Karen watches her, a frown deepening on her forehead.

'And you believe we're in some kind of danger?'

Melanie pulls her sister outside to the street to show her the dust cloud, which must surely be almost upon them. To the east the sky is a cloudless blue bowl. She spins around. Perhaps the tide has changed direction, come around to attack from another side. But the view is clear on all sides. A white bird glides overhead, charting the clarity and goodness of the air in a steady line from North to South. Karen is watching her closely. They need a higher place to look around, she realises. She runs back into the house and takes the stairs two at a time, Karen right behind her. She runs between the bedrooms, stumbling over toys and laundry to look out of all the windows.

'Mel?'

'Shh! Quiet!' she snaps. 'Listen!'

The only sounds are of children playing, someone cutting their grass, the beep-beep of a lorry reversing in an adjoining street. Can they really be safe? She strains to make out the dull roar of demolition lurking under the surface. 'I need to get Matthew,' she says, and starts for the stairs. She can hear him crying and Chloe singing to distract him, but it isn't working.

Karen stops her in the hallway. 'I don't think you're in any state right now,' she says firmly. 'Let me deal with him. I'm going to clear the lunch away, then we're going to have a proper talk.'

Too exhausted and bewildered to continue arguing, Melanie sits on the floor in the conservatory with her head in her hands and listens to Karen smoothing things over with the kids, joking and scolding and clattering dishes around.

Chloe and Nathan must have got over their argument. Nearly all of the Lego pieces have been used to build an eccentric, multi-coloured structure. Part house, part garage, it has ramps and archways, al fresco kitchens and attic bedrooms with tiny balconies. Melanie lies down flat on the floor and peers inside. Little Lego people move along the corridors, smiling. She thinks if she could make herself small enough, she would go and live in there. Take Matthew with her, and maybe they'd not come back. Maybe they would be safe there.

She feels a tug on her hair and there is Matthew, come to find her. His hands are sticky and his face is freshly wiped and shiny pink. He grins at her. His new teeth are like tiny pearls in his pink gums. She hugs him, pressing his small body into her own, breathing in the smell of his hair, his skin, his unquestioning trust. When he gets bored and begins to protest she puts him down and he crawls towards the Lego building.

'Careful,' she warns, worried he'll spoil his cousins' work.

But Matthew picks up a loose brick, then another, puts the first down on the floor and balances the second on top. He looks for her reaction and at first she's lost. Then she remembers herself, and what comes next.

Starting again.

After destruction comes construction, putting one piece on top of another. This simple act defines us. We are the builders. That is who we are and this is what we do. She always knew this but had somehow forgotten it. Remembering now, so suddenly and with such force, feels like something bursting inside her head, releasing the pressure that had been trapped there.

She smiles and claps for Matthew.

He imitates her, smacking his fat palms together and giggling then reaching for another brick, orange as a fish finger. This is important.

Readymade

Elaine was always big on the Domestic Goddess stuff, but horticulture defeated her. When we moved into our brand new marital home, the garden was a patch of thick, claggy clay that didn't drain and refused to support life. She tried her best, shovelling up great wet cubes of clay like oversized pieces of fudge, planting all kinds of doomed green things. She may as well have just taken them out back and shot them, it would've been kinder. As it was, we were treated to the slow but inexorable deaths of dozens of blameless shrubs through the patio windows, drooping, discoloured, dead. The trouble with living things is no matter how hard you try, they seldom behave as you want them to. They have agendas.

Elaine said a lot of things before she left. Hardly any of it made any sense. 'You're empty, Ian,' she said. 'I thought you were all, like, Zen or something. But you're completely hollow. There's nothing there under the surface. Nothing at all.'

Better than being full of shit, I thought, and told her I loved her.

'You don't know the meaning of the word,' she said. 'You don't even know it's a verb, a doing word.'

By this point I had no idea what she was talking about so I told her again that I loved her.

'If you repeat any word often enough it becomes nothing more than a sound in your mouth. You might as well say Labrador or lavatory or, or... truffle!' She shouted that last word at me then she started laughing and shaking her head. 'Ian,' she said when she'd calmed down and was standing in the hall, a suitcase in each hand, 'maybe there's someone out there who's right for you. It is an infinite universe after all. But that person is not me.' She laughed again, somewhat hysterically I thought, and slammed the door behind her. Funny girl.

I convinced myself I didn't need a relationship. The price was too high. But that was before I met Julie. She really renewed my faith in things. I'll miss her.

Maybe Elaine was right. I certainly feel empty now. I don't know how long I've been sitting here in the front room, anchored deep within the armchair. Could be minutes, could be days. Perhaps I'm hungry. Someone once told me that civilisation is only ever two missed meals away from anarchy. Or was it three? No matter. The point is, there are limits. Frankly, I'm amazed there isn't more anarchy in the world considering we're all just a few sandwiches short of mayhem.

I glance over to the corner of the room. A curl of blonde hair disrupts the pattern of the carpet. Such beautiful hair. Julie's lying face down with her legs twisted underneath her, arms flung out on either side. Her skin is still pink. Such lovely skin.

By the clock on the mantelpiece, it's nearly nine. I get up and turn on the telly. Bush fires in Australia, bombs in Iraq, by-elections in Huddersfield. It's impossible to know what to care about. I let it all wash over me. This act requires focus and clarity. The conclusions I've reached, the decisions I've taken, I have not taken lightly. It's a question of following through. To thine own self be true. That means not taking any shit, from anyone.

Outside, in Glenview Crescent, the day leaks away through a hole in the sky after another day of the sun failing to shine upon either a glen or a view for miles in any direction. Darkness slips in over the windowsills and falls to the floor, laying claim to the corners, gathering in the folds of the undrawn curtains. Traffic grinds past on the street outside. You hardly ever see a human being out walking in Glenview: everyone arrives and leaves by car. The whole estate is a machine.

The News doesn't get any better and concludes with a half-hearted report of inconsequential weather wobbling sideways across the country. I'm definitely hungry now. I lever myself out of the armchair and go to the kitchen. Nothing much in the cupboards so I look in the freezer. I have one of those chest freezers, takes up nearly half the kitchen but stores a month's worth of food so I don't have to go out to the shops if I don't want to. It's definitely curry night. Chicken tikka masala with pilau rice and naan bread, it's all there in neat plastic wrappers. A few clicks and pings from the microwave and *voila*. Why anyone would want to bugger around with vegetables and raw meat when you can buy everything readymade, I will never understand.

Julie was the opposite of Elaine around the house – no cooking or cleaning but that never bothered me. Also, she was quiet. Not like most of the women I've known, can't bloody shut up for ten seconds some of them, drive a man mental with their constant yapyapyapping. Julie understood just being with someone, not talking shite all the time for the sake of it. I respected her for that. You've got to have respect in a relationship, or you may as well pack it in.

Things started to go wrong when it seemed like Julie started to lose respect for me. I don't understand how that happened, we didn't talk about it, and it wasn't anything she said. It was that look on her face, that look getting worse and worse until I couldn't stand it anymore, until tonight when I got home. There are always limits, always a line to be crossed. That's been hard to learn. I was always looking for the path of no resistance, without complications and it still pains me to think that maybe I've been wrong. Maybe that route doesn't exist. But if I can think it, if I can almost smell it, then surely it has to? Otherwise, how could it even be in my head? As it was, me and Julie couldn't go on that way and there was no way she was leaving. It's not as if she gave me a choice.

I mop up the last of the orange curry sauce with a bit of naan and try to concentrate on the happy memories, the good times. That's what you're supposed to do when you lose someone, isn't it? But it just makes me feel worse and, to be honest, a little frisky. Not a good combination.

Our sex life was always strong, right up to the end when I would open my eyes and catch her looking at me that way. Before that though, she was always up for it. And she never complained if I wasn't in the mood.

Elaine didn't like it if I woke her up. She was a heavy sleeper so it didn't happen very often but she was always unreasonably pissed off when it did. 'What the fuck are you doing, Ian?' she'd say, pushing me away, and I'd be left high and dry. I don't know what her problem was. A less considerate husband would've raised objections about her always being too tired while she was conscious.

I can admit I was a bit possessive with Julie. We never went out anywhere together. If she minded, she never said. Often when I got home she'd be waiting for me on the settee, dressed in one of her sexy outfits, the French maid or the nurse, and dinner would have to wait. She had this way of balancing her soft little toes on the top of my feet and pressing the whole length of herself against me so it felt like we were fused together, transforming our separate emptinesses into a single beautiful whole. Not some slushy romantic notion of greeting-card love but something elemental, molecular. We mirrored each other, became each other, to the point where notions like love and affection became outmoded, irrelevant. We took each other beyond all of that.

I've got to stop thinking this way. I glance over at Julie again. She's naked. I wish I could, just a quick one. But no, it wouldn't be the same.

I go over and sit down next to her on the floor. I stroke her hair then turn her over. Her face looks so innocent, so sweet, no trace of that smirk now on her lips. I hold her to me. Her body is limp, and so cold and so light. I lay her gently back down on the floor. The gash across her neck lets out a small gasp as her head touches the carpet. I inspect her other wounds, there are quite a few, over her chest and stomach, a real mess. But maybe...

I take the stairs two at a time and throw myself onto the bedroom floor, stretch my arm under the bed and retrieve the box. Tears of relief blur the print on the box but I can still make out the redeeming words – *comes complete with a full repair kit.*

The End of Everything

The button is merciless future-blue and it stares, Cyclops-like, from the lid of the Armageddon Kettle. This is the Terminator of kitchen appliances. Relentless and malevolent, it ticks off the minutes to the end of the world and it *absolutely. Will. Not. Stop.*

From my station in the maze of partitions and screens that make up the offices of SafeGuard Inc, my view of the kitchen area is partially obscured by a plastic fern, so I can't be sure precisely who keeps pressing the button. Every time I pass, I turn it off but someone always switches it back on.

As any broken-backed camel will tell you, there is always a final straw. For this world, that tipping point hangs suspended in the gleaming, pitiless eye of the Armageddon Kettle.

I do what I can. There's not much time.

I reckon I've bought the world a few extra hours with my diligent disarming, but I can do no more without alerting my colleagues, including my boss, to the nature of my mission. Whatever they might make of it shouldn't matter now the world is about to end, but I do need to keep this job. I need to be here. If I wasn't, who would deal with the kettle?

So I click and scroll my days through the company systems, following procedure. I answer the phone and do my best to sound efficient and reliable. Insurance seems especially pointless next to impending global annihilation, but in truth the whole concept has been bothering me for a while now. The plain fact is: shit happens. It will happen to everyone and there is no way of telling which particular pile has your name on it.

One day a small, unthreatening portion, say the approximate size of a Hobnob, may roll into your life. Another day it could be a towering tsunami of effluent engulfs you, your family, your house, your dog *and* your car. The point is, no one gets to choose. And no one gets to stop it.

'I'm really sorry to hear that, Mr Smith. If you can get your completed form to us as soon as possible, we'll be able to process your claim.'

What all the devastated Smiths really want to believe is that their premium is protection against disaster. More than a remedy, they seek prevention: health insurance to prevent cancer; car insurance to prevent crashes; house insurance to prevent weather.

'But I paid all my instalments!' wails the distraught Mr Smith. I picture him like King Canute, on the threshold of his home, brandishing his policy documents as the advancing brown flood water licks at his slippers. All I can do is read from the script presented by the company computers. I can't deviate and say anything more helpful because, 'Calls may be recorded for training purposes.' Which really means, 'Anything you say *can* and *will* be used in evidence against you.'

Customers' reactions to the events precipitating their claims are seldom in proportion to the size of the catastrophe. Some people can bear the loss of their life's work with stoic calm; others break their hearts and cry like babies over ruined carpets. *Carpets.*

The office carpet is bluish-grey, too indistinct to be either one or the other: a blue without conviction, unlike the intense sapphire of the button on the Armageddon Kettle. It glares defiantly at me as I approach, mug in hand. I flip the button up, turning it off and feel a small surge of victory as the blue light is extinguished, leaving a dull, cataract-glazed orb. I take a deep breath and relax just a little, roll my shoulders and circle my head, listening to the muscles in my neck pop and snap like bubble wrap.

No point worrying any more. Stuff like: is there a global capitalist conspiracy, does your neighbour secretly despise you, or is everyone looking at that weird lumpy freckle on the side of your nose? All of these things are now officially rendered meaningless. All of the things you always wanted to do – climb an Alp, learn to unicycle, dance the Argentine tango – don't amount to much of anything when faced with the end of everything.

Travelling to and from the office, I have searched the faces of the people I pass for any awareness of the coming apocalypse. Surely someone else must know what's going on. It's not fair, or remotely practical, for me to deal with this alone. That old man, surely he must realise, as he offers his wife another mint, that the story of their long days and nights together is about to come to a final full stop. The dour bus driver that huffs and grumps at his passengers, scolding them like naughty children; I bet he'd treat them more kindly if he knew he was overseeing their final journey. Or would he simply park his bus in the middle of the street, leave his baffled passengers behind and stride away, making a straight line of the streets to his home and family? Would he throw open the door that no longer needs painting, take his startled-but-pleased wife and puzzled-but-excited children in his arms and hold them, hold them close and breathe through their hair, kiss the tops of their heads and say, 'I will never, ever, leave you.'

Perhaps this happens on another route. On mine, the driver resolutely closes his eyes to the truth and shoves his bus through its gears.

I phoned my mother to attempt some kind of goodbye. I felt I owed her that much. As usual, she knew something was up straight away. All I said was, 'Hi Mum,' and her voice ricocheted back.

'What's wrong?'

'Nothing. Nothing's wrong, really. I just phoned to say hi.' Even my professional phone voice fails.

'You may as well tell me. What is it *this* time?'

The question wouldn't be so dispiriting, even given her tone, if it wasn't for the complete lack of follow through should I be optimistic enough to answer honestly. My mother invariably reacts with an exasperated, 'Well, I don't know what you expect me to do.' Or one of her favourites: 'It's hardly the end of the world!' It isn't what mothers are supposed to say. Not only does, for example, your job suck, or your boyfriend leave, or your dad die, but now you're an emotional incontinent, burdening those who never could do anything to help anyway. So, it's not surprising that when it really *is* the end of the world, I decide, on balance, that Mother is best left in the dark.

I might've told my dad. He may even have believed me, but he's been gone for a year now. Broke his ankle falling off a ladder while putting up a satellite dish, had to go to hospital to have it set and contracted a super bug. 'Necrotising fasciitis,' they said. Fascist bacteria, well-organised and ruthless. I imagined an army of hate-filled bugs wearing colour-coordinated and disturbingly stylish uniforms holding rallies in my father's leg, burning pyres of antibodies before marching on the internal organs, laying waste to everything in their path.

I went back to the hospital the day after he died. I couldn't help thinking about the dirt building up and worrying about the bug he may have unintentionally left behind. What if they didn't clean properly after they'd taken his body away? Did they ever? Perhaps they'd miss a lurking death bug and it would get the next person to use that bed, like the one they missed before, the one that got my dad. But when I turned up with a selection of scouring pads and a bottle of bleach, they turned me away. A nurse presented me with a clear sandwich bag with everything that'd been in Dad's pockets when he was admitted with his broken ankle – £1.28 in change, a screwdriver, a half-empty packet of Victory Vs and a pencil.

So I took everything home and I cleaned there. But I never could get the place clean enough. It did help when Steve, my boyfriend, ex-boyfriend, moved out since he had been one of the main sources of mess. But still the dirt finds a way in. It's a question of vigilance, of not letting your guard down. And hand cream. Lots of hand cream.

'That's the Keep Warm Function. You should leave that on.' Scary Bob's voice is so close it makes me jump, immediately locking the tension back into my shoulders. I didn't hear him approach, but then nobody ever does.

Scary Bob moves silent as swamp gas through the office and materialises at your side without warning. In his position as office manager this is especially useful for instilling a proper sense of fear in his subordinates. A person could be staring into space, picking their nose, updating their Facebook status and then realise Bob is right next to them, and what's worse, they've no idea how long he's been standing there, watching. Has he, in fact, been reading over their shoulder and is now intimately familiar with their online shopping habits? He never lets on. That's where his real power lies – in the unknown. And he knows it.

'But it wastes power. It just sits there and boils, over and over and over again. Is anyone really so busy they can't wait for a kettle to boil? Are any of us really that important?' I'm aware my voice has climbed an octave from its normal pitch and I know I shouldn't say things like this, especially not to Scary Bob.

'It's a feature,' he says and goes back to making his cup of tea, pedantically stirring in far too many clinking circles, like a tone-deaf child given the triangle to play in the school orchestra. When he finishes, he refills the kettle, presses the button down, gives me a warning look and glides silently away.

So, it's him. Bob of the Apocalypse. I should have known.

But still, for now, the world fails to end. I close one eye and fix the other on the blue light, staring it out. The Armageddon Kettle stares back. It has all the time in the world. I wonder, is this really how it all ends? Not with a bang, or even a whimper, but a hollow click and a wet exhalation of steam.

Don't worry. I know what to do.

I make my coffee and flip the button back up, saving the world one more time before heading back to my desk.

Red Bus

I'm picking at the dried curry sauce I just found in my left ear when I step off the pavement and almost get pulverised by a speeding red bus. It goes roaring past no more than an inch from my face, horn blaring, brakes hissing. It's a number thirty-seven, innocently following its normal route, the driver clearly making no allowance for those of us with more on our minds, or in our ears, than that pedestrian preoccupation with life and death.

I'm also on my normal route, on my way to catch my bus to work. Everything is superficially as normal and ordinary as it was a month ago while simultaneously being wholly unrecognisable. The curry in my ear, I should explain, is not normal at all. Or rather, the curry, in itself, as my home-made curries go, is perfectly normal (deep red and not to be taken lightly) but its location, caked around the inner folds of my left ear, is definitely unusual. It must've got in there last night and I mustn't have washed my ears properly in the shower this morning. I can accept that much responsibility but it's entirely his fault, how it got there in the first place. Were it not for him, I am reasonably confident I would not have anything remotely edible in either of my ears.

This isn't the sort of thing that happens when you have your life under control. This thought bothers me far more than the fact of the curry and sends a shot of something hot and fizzy along my nerves, a treacherous cocktail equal parts elation and dismay. I've fallen for the same damn stupid-arsed trick again, that one with the buzzer hidden in the handshake, and can't help laughing despite being absolutely raging.

I walk along to the crossing, press the button for the green man, like a sensible person, and try to piece together the sequence of events.

Last night I was cooking when the phone rang. I jumped, the pot tipped, spilling curry on my hands. I then grabbed the phone, transferring curry to the receiver, and from the receiver to my ear. One mystery solved at least. Although I'm really not sure whether knowing exactly *why* I have curry in my ear makes the fact of it any less ludicrous. It wasn't even him on the phone, just Damian-from-Interior-Life trying to sell me a new kitchen. Poor Damian. He won't be trying that again in a hurry.

He, him, Mr Wasn't-even-on-the-horizon-a-month-ago-for-fucksake, did phone later. He came up to visit, stayed the night and he'll still be there now, in my flat, in my bed where I left him, lying there with his hair all wild and his skin pale gold in the morning light as it filters through the curtains. That image, embedded in the humid atmosphere of last night's sex sent me and my clothes to get dressed in the hall. I couldn't trust myself to behave sensibly. I can't trust myself either, it seems, not to be feeling this way. I'm almost skipping for christsakes, and this idiotic half-drunk smile keeps sneaking onto my face. I almost give myself a slap but decide that's maybe not the right move if I'm trying for a less deranged look.

Not that long ago, I was convinced I'd had enough. Love wasn't worth the inevitable heartbreak when the balloon burst and all the promises and possibilities shredded down to a twisted hard knot. And the long nights spent picking at that knot, trying to understand how it got that way. It wasn't so much that I'd lost heart, more that I'd worn mine out. I couldn't go through all that again and I reasoned there was no real need to. I had friends and family for love and company, and it wouldn't be that difficult to find sex, if I felt the need. Sayonara deep and meaningful. Your arse is out the window.

So now what the fuck am I thinking? *Stupid, stupid, stupid.*

'Look, do you want something or have you just come in here to insult me?' The newsagent looks quite cross and I realise I must've said that last bit out loud.

I mutter an apology and grab the first paper I see, thrust some coins at him, and hurry out of the shop. I am ridiculous.

I tried talking to Liz about it all on our night out last week. We've always been around with an extra box of tissues and catering quantities of alcohol to help mop up each other's emotional disasters. (The ice cream idea is bullshit. Drinking heavily and swearing a lot – that's the thing.) In this case, however, maybe because the carnage hasn't actually happened yet, she was no help.

It's raining hard by the time I get to the bus stop so I go inside the shelter. There's an old woman perched on the narrow strip of metal masquerading as a seat. Her coat and hair are the same rain-grey colour as the painted metal frame. She looks as if she's physically part of the shelter, like a modern day gargoyle. I almost jump when she turns and nods to me. I nod back and take the paper from under my arm, hoping to avoid a conversation about the weather or the eccentricities of bus timetables. She doesn't show any sign of wanting to talk and has already settled back into stony watchfulness.

I sit down and cross my legs only to be pulled up short by a sudden eye-watering tug of elastic. This has definitely gone too far. I've got my knickers on sideways. Easy enough done with those little triangular ones, especially when you've removed the deeply unsexy washing instructions so they don't spoil the general effect, and even more especially when you're too distracted in the morning to pay attention to what you're doing. But all the same. I can feel the colour rising up my neck, inundating my face with the indignity of it all. After all the hard lessons learned, after all the promises I made myself, here I am, snared by my own underwear and helplessly blushing at a bus stop. Ridiculous doesn't even begin to cover it. The gargoyle pays no attention while I not-so-discreetly rearrange matters. She just stares into the rain.

I sit back down, very carefully, and flick through the newspaper. A headline catches my eye, *Hammer time for ex-lover's Ferrari*. The story printed underneath explains how a woman found her boyfriend was cheating on her with her best friend so she smashed up his car with a hammer. I try to imagine finding himself in bed with Liz, just to see if I have any urge to set about his Ford Focus with something heavy, but I just feel a bit queasy.

Maybe this feeling isn't even real.

Black rainwater has formed an ominous puddle which laps at the open mouth of the bus shelter. Cars go skiffing through the edges of it, making waves that only just stop short of the gargoyle's shoes. Still she doesn't move.

Eventually, the blurry image of an approaching bus is visible through the plastic window, bubbled with raindrops. I can't make out the number. The old woman bolts to her feet with surprising speed and leans out into the road as the bus comes nearer. It's travelling too fast. I open my mouth to call her back but it's already too late. The bus comes ploughing up the gutter without slowing down and hammers on past the stop.

The old woman turns towards me and blinks as rainwater streams down her face and drips from her chin. Her shoulders begin to shake and she makes a muffled noise I at first mistake for crying. But she's laughing. It starts with a slow chuckle and builds until she throws her head back and releases this wild whoop of a laugh that goes bouncing around the inside of the shelter like a rubber bullet.

'You live,' she says, pausing to shake herself like a dog emerging from a river, 'but you never bloody learn, do you?'

She's still laughing and I can't help joining in. Then I see, coming along the road, the glowing red promise of another bus, spreading through the rain like a big, stupid smile. I could let it go past. I still can't see what number it is, whether it's the one I'm supposed to take or one that'll get me lost and leave me stranded in some godforsaken place I don't recognise, full of industrial units and three-legged dogs. I could stay right where I am, safe and dry. Or I could step out and take a look.

Story Credits

Worst Case Scenario originally appeared in *Gutter* magazine, issue 8, published by Freight Books in February 2013, under the title *The Heart of a Pig*.

Ladies' Day originally appeared in *Gutter* magazine, issue 9, published by Freight Books in August 2013 and was subsequently reprinted in *Best British Short Stories 2014*, ed. Nicholas Royle, published by SALT in July 2014.

Human Testing originally appeared in *Valve III*, published in November 2013.

Mezzanine originally appeared in *Gutter* magazine, issue 10, published by Freight Books in February 2014.

How to Not Get Eaten by Tigers originally appeared in *Firewords Quarterly*, issue 2, published in August 2014.

Bingo Wings originally appeared in *Gutter* magazine, issue 11, published by Freight Books in August 2014.

Fitting and *Her Feelings About Auckland* were originally published together by *Structo* magazine as a chapbook.

10 Types of Mustard was originally published in *The Grind IV.*

Odd Sympathy was originally published in *Gutter* magazine, issue 12, published by Freight Books in February 2015.

Red Bus, in a longer version, was broadcast on BBC Radio 4 as part of the *Shorts: Scottish Shorts* series in February 2015.

White Pudding Supper was shortlisted for the Manchester Fiction Prize 2009.

Worst Case Scenario (with title *The Heart of a Pig*) was shortlisted for the Bridport Prize 2012.

Home Security (as a single story) was shortlisted for the Bridport Prize 2013.

Thanks

To Adrian Searle, Robbie Guillory and the team at Freight Books for their energy and enthusiasm in producing this collection and for their vigorous promotion of new short fiction in Scotland, not least via *Gutter* magazine, in which a number of these stories first appeared.

To Rodge Glass, whose incisive but good-natured editing made the process a joy and the collection better in every way.

To Nicholas Royle for his encouragement back in 2009 in Manchester, and for choosing *Ladies' Day* for inclusion in *Best British Short Stories*. Short story writers and readers, myself included, continue to benefit from his tireless championing of the form.

To Janice Galloway for her insight, wisdom and extraordinary generosity of spirit.

To the following people for guidance, support, feedback and friendship over the years it took to write the stories that make up this collection. Their fortitude in the face of multiple drafts and hairy canaries has been humbling. It is my good fortune to find myself indebted to: David Hill, Gwinny Gordon, Gail Honeyman, Kirsty Mitchell, George Craig, Dickson Telfer, Martin MacInnes, Bernard O'Leary, Sonja Cameron, Catherine Simpson, Gladys Taylor and Janet Gairns.

To Adrienne and Bill Jarrett for always being there.

To Mike, Andrew and Heather for the love and laughter that keep my Home World turning.